SHATTERED REFLECTIONS

The Reflections Series

Book 1

SK PRYNTZ

Shattered Reflections

by: SK Pryntz

Author's Note:

Please regard the trigger warnings. Your support is always wonderful, but your mental health is more important than anything else.

We all have Darkness in us. I chose to write mine on paper. To everyone living in their own darkness, I hope you find your light.

Acknowledgments

Mom,

From the day I was little, writing about my fantasy worlds, you've always been there for me. Never once have I felt in the dark with you in my life. Thank you for being my cheerleader and encouraging me never to stop knowing my worth (and adding tax.)

Emmy,

I owe you, getting this from notes on my phone to an actual book. Without you and your kind words, I may never have had the courage to give my work to the public!

To my husband,

I don't know where to begin, my love. You have been there as my coach, my supporter, my shoulder, and my partner in crime. All these characters are pieces of us. The story of how my world was filled with darkness, and you have always been the true sunshine letting me finally see. I love you. Thank you for listening until 2 AM, listening to me squeal, cry, rage, and freak out. This wouldn't be possible without your love and support in my darkest times.

To my editor,

Thank you so much for being my rock, my grammar police, my confidant, and my teacher! I love all the nights we stayed up laughing, and I surely wouldn't have been able to do this without you. I never expected to hire an editor and make a friend in the process.

To My Readers

To my readers,

This tale is a dark romance novel about two rival serial killers. Please be advised that the book has multiple disturbing and triggering occurrences. Triggers included:

- Sexual assault (experience in detail)
- Rape (mentioned)
- Somnophilia
- Blood play
- Piquerism (knife play)
- Breath play
- Stalking
- Autosassinophila
- Algolagnia (pain fetish)
- Consensual non consent (Dub con)
- Voyeurism
- Exhibitionism

- Murder
- Torture
- Drug use
- Overdose
- Suicide
- Amputation
- Body mutilations
- Kidnapping
- Gore
- Explicit language

If one or more of these listed is traumatic or uncomfortable for you, my book may not be the best option. If you are still here, I hope you love my psychos as much as I do.

Glossary

Bratva - Brotherhood of Russian mafia

Brât - Brother

CSA - Crime Scene Analyst

Det - Detective

Krasivvy - Beautiful

Malen' Kaya Ten'- Little Shadow

Maya Kayten - Little Shadow

Moya Kotva - My blood

Porthos - Pig

Privyet - Hello

Sestra - Sister

Yakutian - Russian blade

Ya Tebya Lyublyu - I love you

Zaika - Bunny

No One

Leaving Jenni's place, I made my way down the driveway. The fresh air and the quiet of the darkness blanketed me, leaving me with just the light of the moon to guide me. When my feet hit the sidewalk, I began to skip and hum—humming a song from my favorite storybook. Turning the corner, I happened upon a streetlamp that kept flickering, and the strobe effect made me feel dizzy.

Walking over to the damned thing, I kicked it.

Way to be a buzz kill?

Triumph surfaced when it stopped until the bulb started to crackle. I ducked as the sparks flew, and pieces of the broken lamp rained down around me before the world plummeted into complete darkness.

"Damnit," I said, flipping the stupid piece of metal off.

At the sound of an engine, I veered off into the ditch a bit to let them pass. It would be just my luck to get smashed by a truck after breaking the friggin' streetlight.

Turning around, I shielded my eyes from the bright headlights.

What the hell?

I moved further into the ditch, the drainage soaking my

Converse, and I waved my arm, signaling for them to move the fuck on.

They didn't.

The rev of the engine was my only warning before pain engulfed my back, and I was suddenly airborne. I landed in a heap on the other side of the truck, my mind scrambling to figure out what the hell just happened. Two shadowy figures loomed over me. The one on the right popped open the trunk and grabbed me. Fear rushed through me, and I opened my mouth to scream just as the other guy's fist slammed into my stomach. A cloth was pressed to my face, and a strong acidic scent filled my nose. Ignoring the pain shooting through me, I furiously threw my legs out, my foot smashing into the taillight, which sent tiny orange shards of plastic onto the road.

Those fragments were the last thing I saw before my eyes shut.

Chapter 1

Ember

The crimson lines of red streamed down the peddling dealer's body, pooling like a river at my feet. His symphony of screams and pleas was a backdrop to my artistry. I'd snagged him from Carter's street, a known spot for his sort. His bloodshot eyes were bouncing around the empty shipping container.

The outside light was sealed away behind a metal door, and the only items in the space were a dirty metal chair with a cracked plastic seat and me. He would only be able to see a bit once his eyes adjusted within the darkness that surrounded him, but I could see him. Darkness and I were friends. His fear was so palpable I could taste it. It was like an acrid tang in the air that danced on my tongue, and I reveled in the shivers it sent down my body.

As soon as he focused on me, his eyes bugged out.

"You crazy bitch." He spat on the floor, blood coating his teeth. His sardonic grin matched the hysterical tone in his voice.

"Thank you for noticing." I shrugged, but smiled. I'd taken my time with him.

My ears were ringing sweetly from the hours of delicious screaming. The sounds kept ricocheting off the walls, rattling in my head, immensely increasing my enjoyment.

"What the fuck you want?" he said, rocking back and forth and smashing his foot on the cold metal floor like an infant throwing a tantrum.

Rolling my arms around in a circle, I let out a breath. These small fry peddlers were always annoying and hardly useful. This interrogation was going to be a waste of my time.

"Who is your supplier?" I said, hoping the calm tone in my voice would soothe him.

"I ain't know nothing 'bout that." He spat on the floor again, his pitch in tone higher, indicating he was a liar.

I walked closer to him, letting my blade carefully run along his flesh. Bringing my face closer to his, I loved that he still couldn't see all of me. His sweat mingled with the metallic scent of his blood covering him and the walls. The scent was becoming more intoxicating as the seconds ticked along.

"Would you prefer I jog your memory? I hear electricity does wonders for stimulating the brain."

His gulp was audible. I didn't actually have any batteries, wires, or spark plugs to have fun with in this space, but indulging in his reaction was well worth the lie.

"Lady, look…" Ah, yes, the begging had begun. His breathing had picked up, and his body was straining against the binds. "I only give my shit to kids, broke motherfuckers, and tweakers, man."

He was still lying.

His supply had been tainting the cove—the homeless community under the King's Bridge—for a few months.

The crystals were toxic and caused six overdoses in just a week. Nobody ever batted an eye when someone with nothing was killed. Everyone blinded themselves to those they saw as less than human, linking their deaths to that of stray dogs.

"Your shit has ended the lives of a lot of good people." Disgust dripped off my tongue. "You do not have the brain cells to make a grilled cheese, much less create this drug. So I ask again...."

I approached his shaking form, reaching out until his thick, oily fingers were heavy in my hands. His pointer finger was my first target.

"Who?"

Snap.

He screamed, and it was music to my ears.

"Is?"

Snap.

He was louder this time.

"Your?"

Snap.

He whimpered, his hand limp against his side, the breaks of each finger bone jutting out. Smiling, I grabbed his palm, angling his wrist, reveling in the sound I knew was coming next.

"Supplier?"

Crack.

He screeched this time, wildly shaking his head and smashing it into the back of the chair.

"Okay...okay!"

Feeling satisfied, I steepled my fingers together, waiting for the pathetic mess to continue.

"I don't know who makes the dust. It ain't my payroll." He began stammering when I pulled his other hand close, ready to start snapping those fingers, too. "B-B-But...."

He flinched away from me.

"I know the guy I get my stacks from. He's a greasy mother-fucker. He's at the corner of Fulton. Goes by the name Grinder. I don't know nothing else, I swear, lady!"

I pondered that information for a minute. Grinder was a name I'd heard a few times. The idiot got his name by doubling at a butcher's shop. He wouldn't be an easy mark because his stupid pals flanked him like flies on shit.

The dealer was sobbing now. The salty smell of tears invaded my nostrils. Great. He was crying, and I didn't 'do' tears. Ever. I could handle curses from a grimoire, shouting, screaming, anything but fucking crying.

"I helped you, girl. So please just let me go. I won't say nothing, I swear."

This was always the part I hated.

The hope.

It was a bubble of light in the black hole of death.

"Okay, sure. You won't say anything." I shrugged, hearing him sputter and shift around in his uncertainty. "So, take me back to your apartment, then."

His body was hesitant as he flexed his muscles and cradled his battered hand when I released his bindings. He stumbled around, bumping his big body into the side of the container.

"Uh, okay…why?" he said, still unsure.

"Because you're going to use the burner you stash under the oven in your place to set up a meet with this Butcher," I paused, moving in closer. "For this week."

The dealer wobbled in the space. His silence had to be a sign of his shock. He hadn't noticed I'd been tracking him down for weeks. He never detected my presence in his rundown apartment building.

He, nor anyone else, had thought to look around the corners of the noisy alley past the grime-filled dumpsters, dumpsters that happened to have the perfect view into his bedroom. The dumpsters had easily hidden my small frame as I'd moved closer to the window and peered inside. The flimsy cardboard section on his window had been easily removed, allowing me to survey and peruse the area. Once inside, I'd inspected the oven first. The oven was often a hotspot for things to be hidden, and I discovered a small phone concealed inside.

"Yeah, okay. Whatever you want, you crazy motherfucker."

I let that one slide and reached for the handle, opening the container door. The dealer cursed, mumbling and complaining about shielding his eyes from the beaming sun.

Reaching the tail end of my car, I shoved him until he stumbled forward and fell face-first into the trunk.

Once we were inside his apartment, the dealer paced around the space. The smell of molded food and unwashed musky sheets invaded my nose as he walked past me again and again. I scanned the area. Everything was untidy or abandoned. There was a small pizza box on the table. I quickly peeked under the lid…whew rotting pizza.

"Grinder don't wanna meet me." The panic in his voice was palpable.

I figured this would be the outcome. This moron was a peon in the industry. He was going to get more people killed because of that stupidity, not knowing how to cover his tracks or branch out with the poison he sold.

He lived in a studio apartment in the slums. Nobody had bothered to look at his bruised, bleeding body when we'd arrived here. Some had kept their heads down, and others had scoffed in his direction like he'd been the loser in a fight.

He hadn't realized just how badly he'd lost yet.

"Where's your bathroom?" I said, startling him more.

He took me into a small bathroom that smelled even worse than the bedroom. The urine stains lingered around the toilet. Running my hand along the edge of the sink, I could feel the soap scum and dirt lining all the way to the small bathtub that took up half of the closet-sized room.

"Draw up a bath." My tone was not to be challenged.

He hesitated, not understanding what was about to happen, but the flash of my serrated blade put him into motion. It took a few moments for the water to rise to the level I wanted, and then I maneuvered toward him.

His eyes were on me, and his energy felt wary as he pleaded.

"You ain't gotta do this," he said as he stepped into the bath, following the gesture of my hand. I reached for the baggie in the sink and then carefully poured the prepared contents onto a thin plastic sheet the size of a small square.

"You killed six people with your ignorance," I said as my ritual began.

"Thomas Fig, Megan Toomey, Elizabeth Yung, Henry Neth, Richy Bias, and Adam Villa. They had names. They had a purpose. Their blood is on your hands. Your grave will now be theirs to covet."

The blood from his cuts and gashes started to turn the water red. The water's heat was draining his life quicker than I had wanted. Still, I slid my blade along his chest, his eyes watching me in horror. A terrified moan escaped his mouth as I coated his blood on my lips. He continued to track mine as I leaned down and pressed my kiss, my calling card, into his skin.

"You will now drink the poison you gave to them."

He protested and started to back away, but I'd already grabbed his mouth, forcing his cheeks open. Shoving the full contents of his drugs down his throat brought me joy. He struggled against my hold but to no avail. His shattered hand and dislocated shoulder from earlier were working against him. But I didn't care. I craved his pain as I leaned closer to watch his eyes turn red. His breathing became almost non-existent, and his mouth opened and closed like a fish.

He coughed, and the frothy foam oozing from his lips slapped my cheek, adding to my joy at his impending demise. The amount of bubbly saliva grew until it slowly spilled down his neck to his chest and into the tub.

Finally, his body seized. He convulsed as I said the names once more of the lives lost to his poison.

When he stopped flopping around, I admired my brand, surrounded by the man-made toxin.

A mark in blood, a mark in death.

His debt was paid, and another death was avenged.

Chapter 2

Ella

Blood.

So much blood.

I was surrounded by pools of red, watching as they spilled into rivers.

Miles of crude red lapped at my feet, the color darkening to thick, oily tar. I could only watch while my body was pulled under.

I couldn't breathe.

I couldn't see.

I was helpless as the darkness consumed me whole.

I screamed.

Jolting up in my bed, I caught sight of my fluff-ball Persian as she sped off out of the room. My outburst had startled her. I checked the old-school alarm clock as it blinked its neon red light in the darkness.

4:23 AM…

Ugh, these nightmares were brutal. Mitzi was going to put herself up for adoption if I didn't stop scaring the living daylights out of her every morning. You'd think she'd accepted it was our routine by now. Stretching my body and wiping the sweat from my forehead, I trudged to the bathroom.

Work was in a few hours, and I might as well get a head start on the criminal investigation file I knew was sitting on my desk. I replayed the details of the last victim that the unsub had killed as I brushed my teeth.

The victim was a male. He was in his mid-thirties and in the drug trade. Found in an abandoned apartment. Cause of death —overdose.

It was always the same.

Known drug dealer, forced to OD on their own poison. No damn trace left to track down their killer.

Sometimes, we found bloody bootprints leaving the scene, but they always seemed to disappear into thin air. We had run this never-ending goose chase enough times now that we knew to let the rookies have some exercise.

God, my head hurt.

It was throbbing in time with my heartbeat. I desperately needed to chug some coffee to make the annoying pulsing fade in my temples. Granted, it was probably counterproductive, but oh well.

Stepping out of the shower, I wiped the mirror with my hand and stared at my reflection. My blonde hair flopped in a ridiculous manner, and the steamy water didn't do much to chase away the persistent sleepiness from my body either. At least I hadn't woken up on the floor of the lobby or a park bench somewhere random today.

I was an avid sleepwalker, and more times than I could even count, I'd found myself curled up in random spots.

My phone buzzed, almost falling off of my cherry oak night-stand. It was the buzz of a text message.

DET QUINN: Vic at 1266 Carter Street.

Apartment 3B.

See you there.

And just like that, it was back to the grind.

After I made my way into the scene, I scoured through the dingy apartment. It reeked.

Dead bodies usually smelled like spoiled meat, but I had a feeling this place had always carried the scent of death, even before anyone died here. In fact, I wasn't sure that some poor rodent hadn't wandered into a trap somewhere and was left to decay.

Detective Quinn was fussing with his neatly trimmed beard and dark blond hair. It looked even more disheveled than normal.

"The cause of death is either blood loss or an overdose," he said, snapping on a pair of purple gloves and lifting up the head of the man in the bathtub.

His skin looked pale, and I wasn't a medical examiner, but I'd bet he died a few days ago.

"Looks like Snow White struck again." Quinn pointed with his gloved hand.

Sure enough, there was a blood-red kiss lining his collarbone. Upon closer inspection, the mark was crusted over in blood. Per usual, it was confirmed that the blood was the victim's. He had gashes and scrapes lining his marred flesh. He wasn't naked. None of them ever were. The unsub wasn't a sexual sadist. There hadn't been reports showing any foul play regarding sex.

He had on a wife-beater tank top and tattered basketball shorts.

"Do we know if there are any signs of a break-in?" I said, staring at the doorway.

Quinn shook his head, his rough, sleepy tone sounding more tired than he looked. His fancy shirt was untucked, and his suspenders were slightly skewed, which was saying something.

"Nope. The victim let them in willingly."

I nodded, knowing what was going to be said next.

"The victim was an alleged druggie. He'd been reported selling his drugs to some high school kids at Briar. He got away before Bleu could nab him. His stacks snuffed out a bunch of the homeless people. It's not right. Bleu was beating himself up because one of them was a kid at Briar's High."

Micah Quinn was a good man. He always took it hard when kids were caught in the trap of bad people. Their false promises blinded the victims to the reality of what it meant to be in that world, and their poison slowly rotted their marks from the inside out. This unsub always targeted drug dealers, left a bloody kiss on the victims' bodies and killed them with an overdose of their own drugs. That must be why this serial killer was called Snow White.

"Guess it didn't do him any good running from Bleu and the boys did it?" His baritone rumble sounded around me as his baby blue eyes lit up with amusement.

It was rare for anyone to see Quinn's mask of 'Good Boy Detective' falter, his true self shining through, so his smile at the universal justice served had me hiding a grin in return. He was a beautiful man. I had to admit that. His tailored, dirty blond hair faded on the sides, and surfer boy curls fell in front of his eyes. I knew he worked out a ton. Whenever I entered the training center at the compound, he always had gym equipment clanking together.

"What do you make of this, Ella?" I blinked lightly, shaking my head, blushing.

Ogling my partner… I was so lame sometimes.

"U—Uhh…" I stuttered. "I think the perp is our Snow White." I looked over at the dead body. "His name was Desmond Franklin. He was a thirty-two-year-old janitor at Briar High. He was fired last month for suspicious activity regarding his communication with the students."

Quinn was nodding, inquisitiveness covering his face. And dare I say, he was impressed, too? His eyes twinkled with mirth.

"You've done your homework," he said.

"I try to make myself aware of the new peddlers in the area, so that I have a step up when they end up dead."

"When?" He quirked an eyebrow.

Shit.

"Sorry." I bit my lip at my fuck up. "It's just that for the past few years, Snow White hasn't let a drug dealer walk on the street for very long. This one had only been dealing for a few months, and my guess is he got cocky or careless."

He smiled.

It was not funny that these people were dying. Death wasn't funny. It was just that, for once, the ones slipping through the cracks of the system were still finding their prisons or hell.

"Good work, Crime Scene Analyst, Fox," Quinn said, sliding that mask of order and authority back into place.

"Thank you, Detective Quinn." I sighed and smiled weakly.

My phone buzzed in my pocket. Walking away to the small kitchenette area that was being vacated by the crew, I answered.

"This is Ella."

A shrill squeak came from the other side of the line, and I cringed, pulling it back from my ear. A few crime scene team members looked my way, including Quinn. I sheepishly smiled and turned my face into the corner.

"Ella-Ella Bo-Bella...."

"Cassie? Is that you?"

"Banana-Fanna Foe-Fella...."

"Cassie, please, I'm at work," I hissed, covering the earpiece with my palm.

"Me. Mi. Mo-Mella...," she continued to slur loudly.

I rubbed my temple, a migraine forming at the corners and my nausea beginning.

"Damnit, Cassie," I cursed, trying hard to keep a steady professional tone.

Cassie was my older sister, but she might as well have been my child for how she acted. I was twenty-nine, and she was thirty-one. From the day we were kids, I had to be the older sibling and the mother, too.

As a teenager, I was constantly driving to bars at the crack of dawn to pick up her drunken ass or to police stations to waste the little cash I'd made waitressing to bail her out. She was an escort, and turning my head the other way a few times was needed as a criminal analyst.

She had moved a year ago to Syracuse with her shit-stain boyfriend. She hadn't been back to Rochester since then. Well, at least, as far as I knew. I hadn't heard from her other than receiving some disjointed, slurred texts when she had been drinking or butt-dialed me.

So, why was she calling me now?

She was never short on money. Her clientele were all big wigs that I definitely didn't want to know about. There were rumors that even my chief had been one of her customers. She'd been helpful to the station on occasion.

At times, she acted as a confidential informant for the Special Victim's Unit, but I'd heard about her 'good tips' for people of interest.

"Cassie, what do you want?" I tried again.

She sighed dramatically. "Okay, Smella. Fine. You're no fun."

Still rubbing my temples, I waited for her to continue.

"I need your help. Can you meet me at Eastview? I'm in town, and I really need to talk."

"Cassie, I'm working. I'm sure if you need a ride to the mall, you can call Emily or Megan. They probably still have your number."

Cassie started sniffling, her drunken voice going all hiccupy.

"Awe, Foo! You don't understand, Ella. I need help. Not a ride. I need your 'piggy' help."

'Piggy' was what she referred to as my police affiliation, and generally, when she talked about needing my crime scene analyst perks, it had to do with her 'employers.'

Blowing the hair from my face and focusing on breathing, I finally said, "Fine, I'll meet you at Eastview when I clear this scene."

"Thank you, thank you, thank you, Smella! You won't regr—" I cut her off, ending the call.

Ugh, and here I thought a stinky corpse in a rotting bedroom would be my biggest issue today.

The parking lot at the Eastview Mall was packed as usual. I tried to find a place for my little car. After being cut off and cursed at multiple times, I finally found a spot in the very freaking back.

Cassie was waiting at the food court. Her curly, light brown hair was neatly tucked into a bun, which always made her look like a shampoo commercial model. She resembled our mother, and sometimes, it hurt to even look at her.

She spotted me and ran over, her huge platform heels clacking on the loud tile floor as she did. Her arms were outstretched like in those movies with someone at the airport running in slow-mo to their loved one.

Abruptly, she pulled back from hugging me. Her nose scrunched in disgust. "Uh, I know I've called you Smella since we were kids, but girl, you really do smell today."

I covertly sniffed my blazer. Sure enough, it had the odor of that apartment building, and I didn't have to sniff my hair to know that it probably reeked, too.

Damn. A shower hadn't been an option, so my perfume was going to have to do.

"What do you want to talk about?" I ignored her comment.

She frowned, looking disappointed.

"Ugh, you're so robotic. You haven't seen me in a year, and all you want to do is to talk business?"

I saw the flash of hurt in her silvery gray eyes—a reflection of my own—and the guilt set in.

"Sorry," I said, shifting awkwardly.

My feet were killing me from the damned high heels I had to wear all day, and I just wanted to go home, rip off my bra, and eat cheese puffs while watching *Medium* reruns with Mitzi.

"It's okay," She waved her manicured hand at me. "You've been all business since you got a job as a fancy profiler. I get it, and I'm proud of you, Ella. I just thought we could hang out as sisters for a while."

Now, I really felt guilty, and my gaze darted around, landing on her Gucci purse. I guess Syracuse had higher-dime clients? That, or she'd 'moved up' now. I hoped she was okay. I was all for the sex business being a positive venture because even with my job, I was not a prude. I believed that women should get paid for whatever profession they chose.

If that was hustling married, unsatisfied idiots out of their millions, then so be it, but doing it safely was my only concern. I'd worked so many cases that ended with a dead prostitute. The people in power would not think twice about silencing a person if they saw them as a threat.

"You need new clothes that don't smell like rotten fish, so let's start there," Cassie said, knocking me out of my thoughts.

"Uh, sure?" She grabbed my arm, dragging me into the closest department store.

. . .

After about two hours of mindless browsing and hearing her distaste for everything, I was dressed in an emerald-colored floor-length gown. It had a sparkly undertone to it. I felt silly, like an old lady trying to wear a prom dress, but Cassie squeaked her approval and threw my credit card at the snooty cashier lady.

"You're wearing this to the Art Galla on Thursday," she proclaimed, taking the purchase and walking out.

Following her peppy steps, I struggled to keep up. Her long legs made me feel like a Corgi trying to keep up with a Great Dane. She was nearly six feet, and I was maybe five feet, four inches.

"Wait. Cassie…an Art Galla?"

I was not artistic at all. I couldn't draw a stick figure to save my life. I'd mangled my bangs and ruined good clothes way too many times with those convincing YouTube tutorials. Honestly, anytime I saw a fancy art piece, I wondered if a dead body was hidden in it or if there was some huge amount of money plastered inside it for safekeeping. Nope. Artsy shit of any kind was not for me.

"An Art Galla over at Corning—" I was shaking my head before Cassie even finished her sentence.

I wasn't going to some rich college to stare at a wall of random pictures while pretending the artwork didn't look like a child had created it.

"Come on…it will be so fun. They have like a glass-blowing class and even a balloon maker. I want to learn how to make balloon animals so I can dress up like "IT" and scare the shit out of the girls."

"The girls" were Cassie's friends on the streets. I was pretty sure if she'd actually tried something like that, she'd end up shanked. I had met most of Cassie's friends, and they weren't pushovers or frilly at all. They'd all witnessed hard shit in their lifetimes. Many of them were women from battered homes or single moms just trying to make some money to make ends meet.

21

"Pleaaaase…I'm begging you, actually begging, and that's degrading, so like, throw me a bone so I don't break a heel." Cassie kneeled down, gathering the attention of everyone.

So embarrassing.

I was about to say no, but she added a gut puncher. "You know, since you basically abandoned your big sister and you need to show her you even still love her…."

Agreeing to such a barbaric form of entertainment tasted sour in my mouth, so I just nodded in defeat. Cassie squealed and jumped up and down, her platform black heels a deafening sound on the hard tile.

"Yay! Okay, so now let's talk bid-ness." She got serious and changed her behavior so fast that it had me blinking to catch up. "They stole my man, Lenns."

Lenns, aka Lenard, was her idiot drug-slinging boyfriend. I'd heard something at the station about a possible new player who'd come from Syracuse.

Could it be Lenard?

We had narrowed down the vicinity of the Snow White kills. So, we were focused on staying close to that area here in Rochester and not paying attention to Lenns. However, the fact that he was a 'baby' in the drug dealing world and was pulling a Houdini Act made it hard to accept. Cassie's boy toys were not in short supply. They took off within days, hours, or weeks. Lenns had stayed the longest, but Cassie and Lenns fought so much and were only together fifteen percent of the time.

"Are you sure he's not just…." I wanted to say he might just have taken off, but I didn't.

"Cassie, it's fair to say he's not loyal."

"No! My man doesn't step out on me no 'more. Last time he did, I tried to take off his nuts with a butter knife, and let's just say he knows better now."

"Okay, when did you last see him?"

"He just left for a gig. He's getting mad money, so he'll be able to treat me like his little princess. How sweet, right?" My sister hummed dreamily. "But now, he's gone. I got home, and he's been gone for three days."

The Snow White Killer crossed my mind, but I kept that thought quiet.

"Don't worry, I'll run it by my partner and see what we can do to track him down," I said.

"Thank you." Cassie breathed a sigh of relief. "Now…" Her tattooed eyebrows and blushed ruby lips were intent on my face.

I hated being assessed. "What's with the creepy clown stare?"

"When's the last time you went on a date, Ms. Prude?" Cassie's narrowed eyes and half grin told me that she meant business.

Escaping Cassie was no small feat, but I had to in order to go to the shithole that Quinn needed me at regarding a possible drug bust. Cassie said her boyfriend was supposed to have that meeting, and it hadn't taken a genius to put two and two together.

DET QUINN: Fine, Ella, go. But that's a shady place.

If anything weird goes down, you call me.

Quinn's next text said it was a known spot for meets and deals, and that was all I needed to know to go off-book. I didn't want my sister or Quinn roped into all of Lenn's illegal shit.

Finally arriving at the place, I glanced around. It was a diner. A really old diner that must have shut down at least thirty years ago, if I had to guess. Weirdly, there was still a whisper of the scent of pancakes in the air. It could have been my imagination, but the sickly, sweet scent made shivers run down my spine.

It was dark outside, and my shitty flashlight didn't do much to help me see.

I felt blind.

Clearly, this place was a haven for either horny teens looking for a ghost-buster story or maybe just the homeless trying to find shelter from New York's cruel weather. Graffiti, random trash, and disgusting used condoms were littered around on the barstools, the old cracked dining tables, and the rubber floors.

I lifted the creaky part of the bar table, swinging it up on its hinge. I missed my step, and the board smashed down, taking me with it.

"Okay. Noted. Not a friendly ghost, then." I cursed as a plume of dust surrounded me.

Once I finished hacking from the tornado of debris, I assessed my body. Using my flashlight, I could see that my foot landed on a beam about twelve inches down. With my heart pounding, I glanced at my legs, but there were no tears in my slacks, nor was I in pain. I was okay. Truly okay. I carefully used my arms to push my body up and onto my knees. God, that could've been so much worse as I peered back at the significant-sized hole in the floorboards. Shaking things off inwardly and outwardly, I got to my feet. Pushing my investigation onward, I walked back into the kitchen area.

I didn't see a thing except the usual pans hanging over the light fixture and some stale water in a basin. If a deal had been made here, it had to have been successful and long since over. Moving toward the back door that led out of the kitchen, I noticed the broken glass littered around the exit.

Now, it could have been from the kids who had broken in here to get a quickie with Casper as their audience, or it could mean that the deal didn't go as smoothly as it had seemed initially.

I stepped out into the foggy night, my heels crunching on the broken shards.

I better not cut my foot. I swear if I needed to get a tetanus immunoglobin injection from these disgusting tweakers, I will kill them, myself.

After walking about ten feet away from the building, my feet splashed in a damn puddle by the dumpster shoved against the far wall and a Big John Deer green machine. It stunk like rotten meat. There was garbage in there that probably hadn't been touched since the place closed down.

Swallowing the last shred of my decency, I poked the lid of the dumpster with the end of my flashlight, cracking it open. For the second time, swirls of dirt and flies swarmed my face, making me cough and back away. The noise of the falling lip on the moldy metal was as loud as a gunshot.

I cursed and tried to cover my nose from the stench.

Why not add dusty maggot stink to my already perfumed scent tonight?

I steeled myself to look inside the dumpster. What I found sitting neatly on top of a ripped bag made me pause—a bloody serrated knife. The pattern on the hilt of the handle was beautiful, intricate, and a gleaming red color.

Beside it…was a folded origami apple.

How strange….

Glancing to the right, I saw a pile of chopped-up limbs and gagged. Pulling away from the dumpster, I emptied the contents of my stomach. Finally catching my breath, I spat on the ground.

Ugh, disgusting…

God, it was too dark outside. Pulling in another gulp of air, I stared down at my feet. My flashlight aimed at what I thought was a puddle, but I had not stepped into water. No, this puddle was sticky and bright red.

It was blood.

I was standing in a pool of blood.

Chapter 3

Lucius

"Where, oh where, are you going, my Little Shadow?" I tsked in the darkness, watching the painfully annoying but admittedly efficient little killer.

I'd chased her for months, but this was the first time I'd gotten close enough to see her.

However, "seeing" was objective in this instance. All I could really see was some long blondish-red hair and the silhouette of fuckable curves. Or maybe it was just blonde hair, and the red was blood from some dumb fuck who she'd just worked over?

My Little Shadow had me thinking she was a dude for the longest time. Big-ass bootprints always left dead-end blood trails that moved away from her crime scenes, but I'd recently discovered it was just another of the many ways Little Shadow had evaded the cops.

Most glimpses I had of her were blurred or from far away, and nine times out of ten, all I could see was a jet-black hoodie. Baggy and concealed. She was resourceful. I'd witnessed that firsthand. I still couldn't understand how she managed to overpower the dealers she hunted. That was until I saw her last night at that abandoned diner.

She was sniffing out 'Ole Rocky Manning's place. I had worked with that fuckhead in my college days when I'd first fled to America. Rocky was a large ogre of a man. He did not have a single goddamn brain cell and relied solely on mechanical impulses to function. That was back in the day when I gave a fuck and pretended like society's opinions mattered to me.

Rocky was a self-entitled trust fund baby back then, always whining about needing a degree or his mommy and daddy would cut up his credit card. Maybe his parents followed through with their threat because Rocky got into the drug world not long after.

He could just be lying to his fellow 'broke as shit partners' though, while pocketing that shit for extra hookers. Who knew when it came to deadbeat dealers?

Rocky seemed to be having a meeting at that diner with some skinny Mop-Head. This guy was nervous as hell, making his entrance known to everyone around the area with his elephant stomping and cracked-out giggling.

It was clear that someone was hiding in the bushes below me, even with my ass parked far away, perched on the top of the building adjacent to the diner. She hadn't noticed me and my ninja skills. The little killer had been too focused on the ground level as well.

"Rookie." I snorted, shaking my head.

Always look up. You never know when your rival serial killer wants to play.

I watched that dark Little Shadow wait patiently for her kills to approach her in the back.

She had caught them off guard by acting like a limping woman, appearing out of those bushes and shrieking at them. Both the men scrambled like startled rats, running off in different directions. I couldn't keep myself from laughing at the scene before me. How crazy it was to see a frail-looking ball of black terrify two big beef heads.

She couldn't catch both of them. However, Rocky had gone down the alley, hiding behind the building that held my perch. Mop-Head hadn't seen her coming the second time. Her calculated attack was so fast that it was like a blur before my eyes.

She really was like a shadow.

Jamming that needle deep in his throat meant lights out for Mop-Boy, but then she started stalking around looking for Rocky.

How could such a small woman incapacitate two men?

Either she knew she couldn't haul both their lard-asses around, or she didn't give a shit. Either way, the search ended with her walking back to Mop-Head and pulling a square shape from her pocket.

Like some kind of magician's act, the square turned into a big ass tarp. She then rolled Mop-Head onto it and started pulling his body over to her car. Hefting her latest prey into her clown car was a magic act in itself.

I was pretty pissed, to be honest.

The dumb ass pigs had given me a ridiculous name, branding me with the title "The Klaus Killer." Did I look like an old fat man? No. Just because I didn't clean up after myself like my Little Shadow didn't make me resemble good 'Ole Saint Nicky.

My Little Shadow was known as Snow White. It wasn't until seeing her in action that I realized why. I'd chased this girl for nearly a year, and the weapon she used on her victims was always too small or dark to see.

But I could see it now. I wondered what was in that syringe.

Drugs?

Poison?

Meh, I didn't really give a shit, but my tracker stuck neatly to her little blue car. It was easy enough to follow her, so I decided to have a bit of fun while I waited. Dropping down from the ladder of the building, I landed in front of Rocky. After yelping like the bitch he was, he saw my face and started to laugh.

"Oh fuck! You scared the shit out of me. Some motherfucker just came at me and ran off with a new hire of ours."

I yawned, cracking my neck, not bothering to respond.

After a moment of pause, Rocky's smile dropped, and he breathed out shakily, backing up from me and bumping into the stone of the building.

"Well…I better get going. You gotta take care of that club of yours," Rocky said, eyeing the distance behind me.

I didn't take kindly to threats, and the one he'd just let slip really struck a nerve by telling me what to do. He'd left his car headlights on, shining behind my back, lighting me up like a fucking angel. Or, in my case, a fallen one.

"What's the name of your club again?" Rocky said. "Oh right…*Black Mirrors*."

Talk about what's mine, and you just might lose your tongue.

Plastering on a smile, I said, "Oh, yeah, man. Would hate for you to be grounded for missing curfew. Go head on home."

It was a shame I didn't have time to torture that lard ass.

My Little Shadow was heading toward the cove, and it would have been rude of me to delay relieving her of that baby druggie for too long. I didn't have a need for the fuckwit, but after she had snatched three of my kills, I was getting a bit testy. I needed to study her longer before I could kill her, so taking her tweaker would have to do.

"Yeah. Thanks, man. Have a good night." He walked past me, clapping his sausage fingers on my suit jacket.

My control was delicate. It was like fine strands of a rug being pulled slowly. There was an end to it. When it finally snapped, the intricate weave of the carpet was forever changed with each fray pulled free.

I'd reached that point, and fire filled my blood. Rage licked up my spine like a coiled snake, and my muscles were primed and ready to strike.

I took careful steps toward Rocky as he stumbled around in the dark, looking for his keys. He opened his car door and continued searching for the dropped jangling metal on the dirty street. With his back to me and strewing curses, I slid up behind him. With one hard slam of his door, his head exploded with a squelching *pop*. I kneeled on the ground, staring curiously at his brain matter. It looked like pink popcorn.

Yummy.

Lifting the keys with my index finger, I tsked at the giant oaf. Sliding into the car, I tried to close the door. It wouldn't shut, and my rage boiled. Stepping back out, I searched for what in the fuck was blocking the door from closing. I scoffed when I realized it was his half-severed head.

Pulling a kerchief from my pants pocket, I wrapped it around his neck, and with some effort, I finally freed his shoulders from his empty skull. Grimacing and tossing it behind the shabby old dumpster, I shrugged. It was hidden well enough, but it was leaving a river of red under the old metal bin.

My phone blipped, and I could see the tiny dot indicating that my Little Shadow had finally reached her destination. It was a little river by the cove. I never understood why she shacked up with the homeless people. I guess Snow White needed her dwarves.

Was she taking our baby peddler for a swim?

Sighing, I walked over to the dumpster. Something was glinting in the dark.

Well, well, well...

It looked like the little shadow was human, after all.

She even left me a gift. A shiny, serrated dagger was lying on the asphalt. I picked it up, marveling at the intricate work on the handle. It had a red jewel glittering on the end with a crown symbol etched into the metal. A blade must have carved it, but the look of the etching added to its lethal appearance. She was going to miss this.

Hmm…I could use this as an opportunity.

The cops were always breathing down my neck. I was sure the same went for her.

What would the media do if they found her little stabby toy at the scene of a murder?

Feeling the corners of my mouth turn up, I twirled the blade in my fingers. I looked back over at the lump of meat by the car, and my smile widened.

"Ho, ho, ho…."

It was time for my calling card. Reaching into my pocket for the little red paper, I folded the edges over and over as I whistled to the tune of "Santa Clause is Coming to Town."

They wanted to call me the 'Klaus Killer?' Well…How rude of me not to leave a gift?

About twenty minutes later, I found her inside a tiny old boat house, causing wicked trouble. I crooked my neck to watch her through the hole in the broken and tattered wooden slats. Her face was so close to the man who was squawking like a damn chicken underneath her gaze. His pleas made her smile pop. She looked breathtaking in the moonlight.

Maybe it was feeling the high from the fresh kill, but seeing that sexy, carefree smile on the evasive Snow White…it did something to me. God, it made my cock swell. Seeing the little minx work over the idiot peddler was intoxicating. Her tight body poised over him, her Cupid's bow lips asking him the same thing over and over. A mantra, a song, a spell, I certainly felt as if I was under a spell.

"Who is your supplier?" she said.

I didn't know who to feel worse for, the frustrated hunter? Or her sobbing prey?

She must have gotten fed up because as the blubbering fool continued his "Give Me Mercy" speech, my Little Shadow grabbed a plastic knife from a sandwich bag on the ground beside her and began cutting off the fool's tongue.

"The mercy I have given is for my ears," she told the man, picking up his tongue and unknowingly chucking it in my direction.

A squishing sound echoed through the night as the piece of muscle fell to the ground. Picking it up, the pink bloody texture felt light in my hand. Tossing the useless piece of flesh in the water, I looked over at her.

She handcuffed the mute mess to a small cart before slamming her sexy black boot into his face. Once he was passed out, Snow White rubbed the side of her face and closed her eyes. She often got headaches. Using her little hands, she rubbed her temples, moaning.

My cock twitched again, and the feel of her massaging *my* aches invaded my mind.

Wait…No.

The bitch didn't deserve to even look at me, much less stroke me…still, the phantom feeling of her hands made me groan. I glanced down at the placement of my palm. Cursing, I shook my head and dropped my cock as I watched the Little Shadow lay down in her small tent. She had stripped off her bloody clothes and only had on a lacy black bra and panty set.

Naughty, Little Shadow, you're giving me a show.

Slowly sneaking closer to her tent, I bent low and ducked inside her tiny space.

Waiting for a few moments for her soft snores to fill the air, I raised my eyebrow when a god-awful sound arose from her. It sounded like a combination of a Gollum and a dragon, and I swore the tent shook every time she opened her mouth. Damn, she needed to shut up. Smiling, a delicious idea formed as I stared down at my throbbing cock. I knew a few ways to make that happen.

Carefully, I slid my thumb into her mouth. Opening it slightly, I angled her chin up. The pure feeling of her soft skin on my hand made me practically vibrate.

"That's right," I said, staring at her face, lit by the moon. Sliding inside her, I groaned softly. "You should have shut that pretty mouth of yours, because now I am going to fill it up for you. Open wide, princess. Your prince is here."

Chapter 4

Ember

I woke up to the sound of clanking. My little guest must have woken up from his nap.

"Mmmmmrrr fffaa."

Sitting up and unzipping my tent, I swallowed hard. My mouth tasted slightly sour like chlorine. I ran my fingers over my lips, the sensitive sensation leaving goosebumps down my back. Why was my mouth so sore?

Whatever. That was a situation to figure out later. I needed to check on the status of last night's work.

Making my way over to my prisoner, I could see he was still chained up. His handcuffs were attached to a metal boat hook by the dock. His muffled sounds were just annoying now. I'd cut out his tongue when he'd refused to give up the location of his friend at that diner. I hated leaving loose ends, so I needed to go back there and track him down.

Glancing around at my surroundings, I took in the abandoned space. It had been this way for years, and the homeless had taken over.

I wasn't homeless. I could buy some useless fancy mansion if I wanted, but I didn't. By stealing the identities and the credit cards of all my kills, I was able to drain every last drop of currency from their bank accounts. Most of the time, I could snag only a few thousand, but other times, I got ahold of a drug lord or even a higher-up cartel member.

Large amounts of green rained on those days, and even though I didn't give a shit about any of the money, it made it easier to get things done and provided silence. For me, that was most important, especially when situations happened, like the scuffle last night.

Oh, and I'd dropped my fucking dagger.

It was his fault that I dropped it. He ran off like a bitch after my attack, and the continuous clipped whimpering of this nuisance was burning a hole in the memory of gripping my blade.

It was my favorite paintbrush, so to speak. The handle was carved with an intricate pattern of a crown, the end ruby red, the color of the blood I loved to spill.

It had been given to me by my father. He had always loved to call me a princess. He'd hand-carved the metal before he died of cancer. I wondered how he would see me now, realizing I was never the princess but instead always the villain.

The police were no doubt sniffing around and found it by now, so I couldn't chance going back yet. However, I couldn't be left without a weapon. The plastic knife did all right last night, but now I had no way to cut my sandwiches.

About thirty minutes later, I headed toward the hardware store. A black shape ran past me. I followed it into the alley, wary of my surroundings and a strange heat bloomed on the back of my neck.

Someone was watching me.

Out of nowhere, a trash bin rattled on the opposite side of the alley. Freezing in place, I glanced at the metal lid when I heard a tiny "Meow."

"Awe, Hi, kitty," I crooned, walking toward the cute ball of black fur. "Were you the one watching me?"

The sweet little kitten allowed me to scratch behind its ears and make kissy faces. The sweet baby began purring and trying to rub its head into my waist.

Cats were amazing. Animals far surpassed humans, that was for damn sure. The feline followed me into the hardware store, scampering between my legs as I made my way inside the place.

A large biker-looking man was behind the counter, flipping through bills and looking up only to glare at me.

"No hairy little piss-stains allowed in my shop," the man bellowed.

What kind of psycho hated cats?

Ignoring him, I continued to scan the shelf for a knife that at least had a similar weight to my dagger. Sighing and frustrated, I finally grabbed one that would suffice and returned to the counter. The balding man had sweat pouring down his face and smelled like old cheese. He leaned in close, and his breath smelled even worse as he narrowed his eyes at me.

"I said, no hairy—" he started, but I slapped my hand over his mouth to silence him.

Surveying the area quickly, I noticed the store was empty, and the camera on the far back wall was a fake. Placing my purchase on the counter, I latched onto his shirt collar and pulled him in nice and tight. This guy was a slob. His orange shirt had ketchup stains on it, and his belt was digging into his gut, lifting his shirt just enough to reveal hairs poking out of the stretched skin covering his belly.

"I know what you said," I stated, remaining calm.

He shook his head free and said, "So, get that tiny piece of shit out now, or I'll add it to my collection of taxidermy friends behind me."

He gestured behind his desk to an array of dead, stuffed animals. There were small and big animals, from rats and foxes to bison and lions.

So he was a poacher, a hunter, a killer…

The corners of my mouth lifted into a slight grin, and I raised my gaze until I felt the tip of his nose on mine.

"Very well," I said.

Yanking on his shirt collar hard, I slid his large, sweaty, disgusting body over the counter and grabbed the man's belt, ripping it from the loops. His pants fell to his feet, and he blinked in surprise.

But I grinned wider.

I snagged the blade from the counter in front of him. With one swift motion, I grabbed his pathetic penis and sliced it off, letting it fall to the ground. The damn thing felt like a shriveled-up raisin.

He screamed, buckling to his knees. He tried to stop the blood flow with his hands streaming from his crotch, but it was useless.

Bending down, I stabbed the inch of flesh off the carpeted floor.

The man, I mean sobbing mess, could not remove his hands for fear of bleeding out, so it was easy to shove his pitiful dick into his mouth. Slamming my hand over his mouth and nose, I blocked his airways until he had no choice but to swallow what had been given to him.

"There you are. Just as requested. The hairy piss-stain has been removed." Sliding back over the counter, I beamed.

The scent of horror wafting off of the dying man gave me goosebumps. Again, I peeked at all the taxidermy behind him. There were so many animals there. Animals that were killed for their fur, meat, or sport. Their lives snuffed out by this man. The bastard probably laughed as he watched them suffer until they finally felt the mercy of death.

Well, now they could stare back into their hunter's vacant eyes, knowing that he'd become prey in the end.

When I returned, the sniveling druggie wasn't where I'd left him. The handcuffs laid open on the cemented ground by the docks.

What.

The.

Fuck.

I sauntered under the bridge, arriving at the cove. Most of the community was busy, but when they caught sight of me, they scurried away like rats. When I finally reached the torn black tent I had been seeking, I found Randall.

He was a sweet kid who didn't deserve the life he'd been given. He was an educated twenty-year-old boy. The life of homelessness came to him when his older brother, Trevor, was found in their flat with a knife wound in his chest and obvious remnants of a drug overdose.

That was one of the first kills the cops tried to pin on me, but I didn't kill without a cause. I also didn't kill teenagers that were getting high. I didn't want the 'factory worker' who was curious about how "the machine" worked. I wanted the builder of the factory, the CEO, and the whole corporation of companies who allowed this type of behavior to happen.

Randall knew what I was.

He was probably the only one who was not afraid of me. At

times, he had helped cover for me with law enforcement. During others, he'd helped be my ears for any new peddlers slinging around poison.

He wanted to see the end of drug dealing as much as I did. But Randall was a good boy. He tried to see the best in people but was easily swayed into believing a sob story or the hope of redemption for evil.

I jiggled the zipper of the tent. The action was like a knock on a door, a polite way of greeting. Randall came outside, his springy black hair bouncing as he waved warmly to me. There was a slight sheepish way he grinned, and I knew he was hiding something.

"Funniest story today, Randall," I said, my arms crossed over my chest.

"Yeah? Well, I have a sorta funny one, too, Ember."

I raised my eyebrow expectantly. Sure enough, he pulled the back tent flap aside, and there was the baby drug dealer huddled up in a ball, sipping water from a canteen.

"I had to do something, or he was going to alert the cops," Randall said. "All of his squawking and rattling of the metal…. We all heard it from under the bridge."

I let out a breath, annoyed at the predictable nature of my friend.

"You gotta be more careful, Em." he chided, shaking his head and running his hand over his clean-shaven jaw. "We got pigs acting like they give a damn lately because of all the ODs. There was a nice guy who talked to us. Detective Quinn, I think that's what he said his name was. Solid cop. Nothing like the dirty ones I usually see."

"Any cop, nice or not, is no friend of mine." I was not going to be challenged on this matter. "And pampering the scum I need to question isn't going to make "friends" with me either."

The hurt rolled off of Randall's being, and his form slumped. His big milk chocolate eyes narrowed.

"Yeah, well…" his deep voice began. "How 'bout you? Stop being careless and only thinking about yourself. You're bringing these people down here. Did you ever think you could be the reason the other tweakers come here to sell their shit?"

Now, it was my turn to feel a slice of tangy pain. I schooled my features, not wanting my anger or hurt to shine through.

"I do not need you telling me how to do business." I scoffed. "You couldn't keep your own blood safe, and you think you can keep people who are viewed as stray animals from harm? Don't fool yourself, Randall, or you'll be the one ending up in a morgue with Trevor."

The betrayal washed over me like ice, the hum of his being sending daggers into my cold heart. I didn't wait for a reply, though. Instead, I grabbed the dealer by his shirt and hauled him back under the bridge. I ripped the canteen out of his hands, tossing it aside.

I was fuming, frustrated, and hurt. The one person I actually liked in this shithole world just turned against me. I saw Randall as a little brother. I basically raised him when he came here. Carelessly pulling the idiot dealer along, I reached the docks again. Tears stung my eyes, feeling annoying and foreign.

I faced the water and heard the icy river licking the dock, splashing frigid waves onto the concrete. Kneeling down next to the jerk, I heard an odd crunch under my knee and saw a piece of red paper-like item on the ground. My hands stalled from shoving this low-life into the murky depths.

The item under my knee was a folded piece of paper in the shape of an apple. The delicacy was strange in a rundown place like my home. I licked the paper. Some thick blood and oil were on the edges, and there was a word written in the middle.

Opening the folds, I read aloud, "Sweet dreams."

A sharp sting slammed into the back of my head, and my vision went black.

Chapter 5

Ella

Being called to the station at the crack of dawn was frustrating on a good day, and I had not been having the best week. I'd awoken in the middle of the street at three in the morning and only had about four hours of sleep.

I had a pounding headache, too. My migraine today was even worse than usual. That was until my cursed phone made the pounding and throbbing more intense.

"Hello, Detective." The annoyance in my voice was evident. Trying not to wince at Quinn's raspy, sleep-filled tone was almost impossible.

"Yeah, I know, Ella. I'm not thrilled either."

The chief was an asshole, plain and simple, for demanding overtime, and whatever was happening at the station made him even more fun. Most of my absences lately, I'd blamed on the chief. There were only so many times I could be summoned to do someone else's 'bitch work.' On top of that, the perfect-Emily made sure the chief knew about any time I was late.

Was this why he was making me take a missing person's case?

The chief never called me. He just barked orders in a text

message or sent his lackeys to get my ass and take me wherever I was needed. I didn't deal with any cases not related to the Snow White killer. He or she had enough kills to keep me busy.

"Why does the chief want me for a missing persons case?" I was confused as to why I was even having the conversation.

It was very clear from the old diner that the guy was killed. Hell, he was gift-wrapped for us by someone with a passion for murder. It was not the usual modus operandi of Snow White, but a serrated knife was found by the mangled corpse. Plus, DNA had linked that weapon to at least five of the last victims, including the chopped-up boy in the dumpster.

The profile for this unsub was all over the place. Sometimes, the evidence led to this individual being male. Sometimes female. Bloody bootprints were found, leaving every scene, and they were a size ten or ten and a half.

I couldn't imagine a female having feet that large, but it was possible. Other times, the height of the unsub was suggested to be around five feet, four inches tall, which again could be a male. But, the blood splatter from certain knife wounds on the victims looked more strained, like the unsub had to put a massive amount of effort and weight into their slicing motions.

Despite what movies and TV shows presented, the human body wasn't this thin paper material. It was difficult to cut through it, especially to the bone, which Snow White liked to do.

The whole case was as confusing as ever. For years, we'd chased down Snow White, and I kept looking more and more incompetent at my job with how many twists had been thrown at me.

There was never a specific reason for a kill other than some affiliation with drugs, and not just one specific drug had been singled out—the killer focused on all of them.

The last victim overdosed on meth, but there were too many

other possibilities: heroin, cocaine, high doses of prescription-style narcotics, and pain stabilizers. Every victim also had trace amounts of the same heavy sedative in their system.

That part at least made sense. Now, whether or not the Snow White killer was male or female....

This unsub liked to pick fights with the most giant meatheads of men. If this killer was a female, I couldn't imagine she would fare well in a hand-to-hand combat situation. Plus, at least so far, Snow White was too calculated to be caught off guard.

"What is waiting for us when we head back in?" I said.

"I'm not sure. Maybe it has to do with that uh...crime of passion from earlier," Quinn said.

I could hear Quinn trying not to cringe through the phone. The scene today was disgusting. A local hardware store owner was mutilated. I didn't particularly like the guy. He had trophies of dead carcasses hung everywhere, and I still was enraged about the hundreds of animals he had caged in the back of his shop. Poor things had looked terrified. We rescued about twenty cats, one hundred rabbits, ferrets, rats, and four dozen reptiles.

My stomach still crawled from the rescue team's words about just how mistreated those poor souls were. Not every life made it out, but a lot did. If I were honest with myself, I was glad that disgusting fuck died because someone chopped off his dick. We never found the appendage, but I had a feeling we may be lucky.

"Okay, Quinn. I'm on my way," I said, hitting the end call button on my phone.

The station was like a second home to me. I didn't know why I felt such a sense of dread walking in now. Maggie, at the front desk, smiled at me. "Hey, Ella. You look beautiful. Did you curl your hair today?"

The answer was no. I just hadn't straightened it. My hair was a pale yellow, springy mess that looked like a lion's mane. Put that hair next to my super pale skin, and I looked like a pale oddball. I used to get called Banana Head or Casper all the time in grade school.

At least those qualities made dressing up like a zombie on All Hallow's Eve easier. My dad used to love dressing up with me and my sister. Most of the time, he drove us around, not feeling up to participating in Trick or Treat adventures. But a few times, he went all out. He was even the king to my princess one year.

I missed my dad.

He was the one person in my life I'd loved so much. I was such an awkward person. Cassie was really all I had as far as friends went, and she was my sister who was blood-bound to love me, so I doubt that counted.

"Chief Doger asked that you try to get something out of this guy." Detective Emily sneered at me.

Emily liked me as much as a mean girl from high school liked a new student. I was someone to pick on at every opportunity she was given. Emily got a 'golden star' for knowing how to torment me, which included ratting me out for being late a few times.

"Uh, okay," I said, wanting to scream at her.

Turning away from her, I peered through the glass at the banged-up male in the interrogation room. He was shivering so much I could hear the faint sound of the chair clicking off the hard ground.

He looked like hell.

His eyes were blackened, leaving big purple bags on his tanned skin. He had cuts and scrapes lining his arms with bandages that already had a red tint to them, and his fingers were twisted at odd angles under a cast. There wasn't a single time Snow White had allowed someone to escape, but this guy definitely fit the profile of one of Snow's victims.

Maybe the notorious killer finally slipped up?

His brown eyes darted around the room, looking crazed. It made me wonder if he was detoxing cold turkey from some hard drug.

Frowning and smoothing my green blazer, I looked at Quinn to tell him I was ready. We entered the room, and the man at the desk ignored us, his eyes still bouncing around frantically, the chair vibrating with his shaking.

Quinn stood by the chair, and I sat down, trying to put myself on his level. He was already acting like a startled deer, so I was afraid to push him because I knew he was likely to lose it.

"Excuse me," I said, gently placing my hand next to his on the table.

His eyes finally met mine, and his already crazed gaze turned horrified. The man absolutely lost it. Something equivalent to a scream escaped his lips, and it stunned me as I caught a glance inside his mouth.

His tongue was missing.

He started frantically pulling at the chains, bashing his already broken hands on the table to loosen them from the cuffs.

With my eyes wide, I slowly raised my hands in surrender. Quinn lunged toward the man, trying to restrain him from harming himself or me. His barbaric screeching and lunging at me made it clear that was indeed this man's intent.

"Mmmmmrrrr fraaaa oooo!" the man screamed at us. His words were incoherent, which made sense with his missing tongue.

"This is pointless," Quinn barked, smacking the wall and motioning to the two-sided glass at Emily. "This man needs a psych ward and a prison cell."

I awkwardly stood near the corner of the room, trying to

distance myself from the flailing man. After an hour in a cell, some doctors and a psychologist hauled him away.

"Are you okay?" Quinn held my arms and rubbed my shoulders, his face showing all kinds of concern. "Your hand, your arm were so close to his." He grabbed my wrist to assess if I was injured, flipping it around until I lightly pulled away.

"He didn't hurt me. I just startled him, I guess." I forced a tight smile.

"Don't blame yourself, Ella. That man was unhinged from the get-go," Quinn assured me. "He acted like a tweaker, and whatever he was on made him a complete nut. You didn't deserve that."

It was not the first time I had people freak out when we went to interrogate them. A lot of these drug dealers were just off. Plus, Quinn was right. 'Taking it personally' was not part of the job description. I knew that, but I always felt sad that I couldn't offer them some type of comfort. Drug dealers were horrible, but no one should endure what that man had.

"Scare another one off already?" Emily said. Her prim, frosty smile was as fake as her boobs.

Quinn frowned at her, but I ignored it. His phone rang, and he gave me an apologetic look before moving aside to answer it.

Emily took no time to start in on me. "Is your superpower making everyone you talk to turn into a mental patient?" I would never understand why she loved to poke at me so much.

"Maybe because you're certifiable." My jab did not phase her even a bit, but I continued. "The suspect's hands are incapable of writing, and his tongue was cut out. There was nothing we could have gotten from him."

She scoffed, fussed with her bangs, and flipped her red hair into my face with a flick of her wrist. Emily was beautiful. She looked more like a model than a detective. Everyone, male or female, fawned all over her, except for maybe Quinn.

She had fake boobs and mostly a fake face. All her clothes were brand names from Gucci to Armani. Whereas, I always wore Goodwill slacks and a camisole with a different color blazer each day. I didn't like flashy clothes, and even the stuff I did wear always felt itchy.

What was it with some of these detectives looking like they made a ton of money?

Even Quinn dressed to the nines. His white button-downs always looked so silky that they probably felt like a cloud on his skin. His black suspender and jacket suits were very Ken doll-esque. I always wondered if he would eventually succumb to Emily's evil-fake charm and marry her. After all, they looked like they belonged together.

"That was the chief." Quinn walked back to us, and his formal, robot-cop voice was in full swing. "He said a witness saw our missing person at the homeless community under the King's Bridge."

"That's great, Mickey," Emily purred, her plastic tits pushed up against his chest. "Don't bring Ella there if you want anyone to talk."

It drove me crazy that she mangled Quinn's first name. It was Micah, not Mickey. I openly glared at her as she giggled. Quinn awkwardly laughed and stepped back from her perfectly manicured claws.

"Ella is our profiler, and this missing person case is linked to our unsub," he stated. His tone was flat as he pulled my arm gently away from the sneering bitch. Emily's gasp made me giggle as I let Quinn drag me to the elevator.

"She's rotten to the core," I mumbled.

Quinn chuckled, blowing out an exasperated sigh. "No one has called me Mickey since I was in diapers, and the last person to do so has an empty grave."

I gave Quinn's shoulder a squeeze. His sister, Penelope…her death was hard on him. From what I was told, he had gone off-grid for months, and they never did find her killer. I couldn't imagine how that felt. My sister was an annoying pain in the ass, but I'd be truly lost without her.

The elevator dinged, and I waved to Maggie as we passed her desk. I noticed Quinn looked a bit sheepish and hid behind my short frame, which was ridiculous considering he was six feet, two inches tall. It was equivalent to a fox hiding behind a giraffe.

"Uh, why are you hiding from the only sweetheart we work with?" I said as we walked to the squad car.

"Uhm, well…." he said, fussing with his neatly trimmed beard.

I'd known him long enough to know this was what he did when he was nervous or angry. However, I couldn't picture why Miss Maggie Cline would make him feel either of those emotions… unless it was romantic?

I raised my eyebrow at him.

"Did the notorious Micah Quinn break the heart of good little Maggie Cline?"

I was dumbfounded, honestly. Quinn kept to himself, and he wasn't known to date. Everyone drooled whenever he was around, and I swear, any man or woman at the shop would've given up their firstborn to converse with this gorgeous man. But the prince simply didn't want a princess. Sometimes, I thought we were only close because he initiated a big brother relationship with me. It made no difference because I wasn't looking for Cupid to interfere with my busy life.

"I, ah…." Quinn's cheeks turned red.

I laughed, shaking my head and getting into the passenger seat. "Say no more. Your business is yours, partner."

He audibly breathed a sigh of relief and started the car. I was curious, though, about what had happened, but we had more important matters at hand. Maybe we would finally catch the Snow White killer.

The homeless community was such a sad place. A huge pang of guilt lanced through me at seeing the conditions my fellow humans were forced to live in.

It was awful.

No, more than that—it was wrong.

Our world had too many things backward, and letting people sleep on a moldy underpass at the King's Bridge was by far the biggest offense.

We walked silently along the rows of tents and people. The grounds were littered with trash and tattered clothing, and no one would even look in our direction. Some would catch sight of us and run off like sewer rats.

The tents all lined the area, which led to an abandoned dock. There were no boats, and besides one tent, there wasn't anything here.

Why is there only one tent back there? That looks lonely.

"Looks like it was a false alarm." Quinn sighed, trying yet again to get a homeless person to speak to him. The shredded clothing of a man snagged on a rock as he tried to run, but he couldn't get away fast enough.

Why were these people so afraid of police officers? It was heart-breaking.

Quinn left to find the male to ensure he had not injured himself from the hasty retreat, so I kept walking the perimeter.

Coming across a red tent, I peered inside. A black man was eating some dry ramen noodles and reading a book. He didn't run away when I approached him. No, instead, he flipped me off and told me to get the fuck away from him. I didn't understand why the hell this particular group of people was so rude and skittish.

Geez, it was like we wore repellant. Admittedly, I knew we'd failed these people, and if I owned one of these tents, I would hate us, too. Quinn met up with me, and still, not a single person was willing to speak with us. We had no reason to keep bothering anyone here. Chalking it up to a false call, we gave up and went home. At least Mitzi would have some company today.

I made my way home from the station, walking away from the hardware store and a ton of yellow tape. Cringing, I decided to go through the back alley of the building instead of walking in front of it. My apartment was just a few blocks from here, and I had my police-issued gun with me, so I doubted any fool would be dumb enough to try and rob me.

As I walked through the dark alley, fear flooded my body.

Why did I go this way?

Old scary movie scenes kept running through my head, knowing I was the dumbass walking toward the bogeyman in the scenario.

A flash of black skittered past me, and I screamed, falling back into a dumpster. Unholstering my weapon and blindly waving it around, I finally paused and opened my eyes. Perched beside me, without a care in the world, was the cutest black cat. He looked like a little shadow because he was entirely black. Even its eyes looked dark.

"Awe, Hi, little kitty," I said, scratching the little ball of fluff and allowing him to jump in my arms. He acted like I was his best friend.

Was he left here from that psycho's chop shop?

I frowned, glancing around but not seeing a single person in the area. My heart felt heavy for this little soul. "Welp, it looks like you found a new home, my little batboy."

He ran around in circles around me, seeming to understand my words. Sure enough, as I kept walking, he followed alongside me. I smiled sheepishly, thinking of the less-than-enthused Persian feline already in my apartment. It looked like Mitzi had just become a mommy.

Chapter 6

Lucius

I sighed irritably as I sat in the far corner room of the club. The redhead bouncing on my dick made me feel absolutely nothing. Her cries of pleasure and passion as she got off for the fifth time only increased my annoyance.

I could not stop thinking about my Little Shadow.

How did she manage to evade the cops so easily?

I had planted that meat sack so perfectly with her knife, making sure the notorious Snow White was placed at that scene. Then, I tailed her to the cove, and after giving her a much-needed clock to the head, I stole her little toy and released him right at the police station.

It took an hour of sweating my ass off in those bushes, waiting to see the whole brigade of cops swarming to get the little blonde fiend. But no, instead, I saw a sobbing mess being hauled off in a straitjacket.

It was very rare that I didn't get what I wanted. I'd spent a lot of time and money to ensure I always had anything I was remotely interested in trying within reach. Anger boiled beneath my blood. I pushed off Callie or Chloe or whatever her name was and snapped up my pants.

"Hey," she protested, spluttering on the ground.

I didn't bother giving her a second glance because I didn't want her anymore…I wasn't lacking in women begging for my cock, and I liked to have my pick. I grabbed my button-down shirt and left the room. The booming sounds of the club's music vibrated over my skin, and that tangy scent of sex and sweat coated me like a cologne.

Damn, Little Shadow, damn the police for being idiots, and damn me for not shoving her in the water when I had the upper hand.

Why the fuck didn't I do it?

The woman was the bane of my existence. I hated her, and she fueled my rage to an inferno level, but something about her calculative nature made me want to face her head-on. It was a challenge of a lifetime, and I wouldn't waste a perfect game by cheating the other player. I wanted to revel in her failure, watch her face as she saw me defeat her, and feel her sweat and blood coat my hands. Hopefully, I would finally shake off the humming, buzzing sensation her addictive smile created in my body.

"Heeey," a drunk bimbo purred at me, plastering herself to my chest.

I swear, these slutty females were such a pain in the ass. This particular one I'd fucked three days ago, and her slurring and panting made it apparent that she wanted more.

"Remove yourself from my arm, or I'll do it for you," I said, feeling distaste crawling up my body.

Why do some people have no respect for personal space?

My tone must have had enough of an edge to it to sober her up because she let go with a sob and ran off. Good, she could console the other female she was with, Cameron, or whatever. I walked to my bar. Guto and Sam masterfully used the Boston shaker and strained the rocks into margarita glasses. Guto caught sight of me and smiled his expensively whitened teeth in my direction.

"Hey, boss. Want your usual?"

I nodded. "Yeah, give me the bottle."

Guto whistled and handed me the Russo Baltique, my favorite liquor from my home.

"Rough night, my man?"

Guto was a kind Brazilian guy. He had worked for me for years, and he and Sam kept things running smoothly. They were both good-looking people, and they had their fair share of fun with the patrons and partygoers. I didn't care one way or another if Guto got his dick wet as long as my bar was staffed and some of the idiot women, who were doused in so much perfume I couldn't breathe, were taken care of and left me alone.

"You could say that." I shrugged, knocking back some of my favorite vodka that reminded me of Russia.

"Hi, boss, how was your night?" Sam came strolling over, her delicate creamy hands shaking some man's drink. The dude was leaning so far on the bar to get a view of her ass that I was surprised he didn't fall over.

I smiled at Samantha. She was a beautiful soul. The kind of person I sometimes wished I could be. Her short, bouncy black hair and curvy body always made me happy. I would never fuck her, though. I didn't mix business and pleasure, not that I got much pleasure from sex. Sex was more of a mechanical need to 'oil the motor' and keep me somewhat cooled off.

I never understood why people made such a big deal about sex. It did nothing more for me than a good workout could get me.

"Good evening, Samantha." My words always made her blush.

She told me, more than once, that my accent did things to her, and I guess she wasn't lying because she was batting her thick black eyelashes at me. Winking, she giggled and went back to her customers.

Sure enough, that horn dog that couldn't get a good enough view of her nice ass eventually fell off his barstool, smashing into the bar table. The dumbass busted his lip.

A bunch of people gasped and fussed over him, Samantha being one of them. She ran over to the corner, snagging the first-aid kit. She pulled out some ointment to help the fool.

I watched with disinterest as she dabbed his lip with a cloth and applied goop to the wound.

I was about to turn away when the sorry, sad sack decided to grope her, her discomforted squeak barely audible in the chaos of the room.

Seriously. What was up with the handsy fuckheads tonight?

I hated when anyone decided they could just up and take what was not offered to them. How manly did you want to feel to overpower a fucking woman? I slid off my stool, gripping the forty-thousand-dollar bottle of vodka in my hand. Sam was laughing nervously, trying to pull her hand from the fat fuck, when I smashed the bottle into his head, knocking him out cold on the ground.

My bartender shrieked, scampering off behind the bar, along with about a dozen other patrons, who freaked out and charged for the door. The pathetic waste of skin was unconscious at my feet. He kicked at my need to kill, but so many people were looking in my direction.

I growled and walked over to one of my bodyguards, Mario.

"Get this disgusting asshole out of my club," I said.

Some blood slid down my arm. That was when I noticed my hand was cut. It was probably from the glass, so I snagged the first-aid kit Samantha left on the bar and found some gauze. The fact that I needed to wrap up my hand annoyed me.

Checking back in with Mario, he grunted and nodded at me. The man was a wall of muscle, but his grunt of confirmation that the situation had been 'handled' was our only form of communication.

Good enough for me.

Later that night, I ran into Javier Ramirez. He was a nervous mess. He paced back and forth, leaving a hole in the floor from his consistent movement.

"I do not know, man, I'm telling you…." Javier started. "The cops just wanted me to be a fucking snitch. They kept asking who the Butcher was, but I swear I will not flip on Markus."

My fingers twitched with the need to draw blood, and it was growing more intense by the second. I had to calm down. This fool was currently working with the cops, and killing him would only cause the soles of my shoes to wear down from having to get farther away from those nosy-ass pigs.

"Get the fuck out of here," I ground out, rubbing the bridge of my nose. "Listen to the law enforcement exactly as they say, and report back to me when they get in touch again. Use your burner only."

The mule didn't waste time. Maybe he could feel the heat of my aggravation because it was radiating off me.

God, if I didn't kill soon, I was going to lose myself.

Stalking toward an alley, letting the shadows hide me, I ducked under the bridge and found exactly what I was seeking—the first tent under King's Briar Bridge.

"What are you doing here? I don't know you, man. Keep

walking on." The young man's springy, black hair bounced with the slightest movement.

I simply smiled, that fire licking up my arms and consuming me bit by bit.

"Of course," I said, eyeing the friend of my Little Shadow.

He was standing in the tiny corner of the tent city. All around us, lined, side by side, were tattered tents and sleeping bags, most closed for the night, which made sense because my watch said it was close to four in the morning.

I wondered why the kid was awake. Snow White called him Randy or something like that. I continued my walk, getting further in and finally under the bridge. The noise was deafening when a car drove over, and I wondered how these people slept.

I wonder if my Little Shadow caught any more prey.

The feeling of being near her little area of tent city had me buzzing. Electricity sizzled and hummed underneath my skin.

Arriving at the dock area, I looked around, trying to find some shadows to hide in, but there weren't many. In fact, there wasn't much of anything in this area at all, just a tiny little blood-red tent. The falling water from the release valves attached under the bridge echoed as it dropped into the water below and onto the damp concrete.

It was pretty damn dark in this area, and I wondered how the fuck the girl hadn't fallen to her death in the frigid water because of the lack of light. I had to make careful movements to be sure I wasn't doing her a favor and ending myself.

If I had to guess, the cemented block of concrete was about six or so feet up from the water, and even with the low tide, I doubted very much I'd be able to find that flimsy ass ladder I'd hidden on before when I waited for the right moment to make my move.

I listened in the darkness, my eyes straining to catch the small bit of moonlight that periodically filtered through the cracks.

Damn, this woman was a fucking bat. No wonder she could hide so easily from the law, but she couldn't hide from me. I approached the tent, careful with my footfalls. Picking up a broken bottle, I used its reflective properties to help me see by using the moon's light.

Was she sleeping again?

The realization that I was so close to her and that she was so helpless and unprepared had sparks of adrenaline popping around inside me, making it easier to see in the dark. Unzipping the tent slowly, I squinted hard, listening for soft breathing or rustling. Anything to show I had alerted her.

Instead, I was met with an empty tent and stale air.

Snow White wasn't with her poor dwarfs tonight.

Interesting.

I crouched down, cramming myself in the small space. My size made this tent look like a clown car. My knee jammed into the corner of something hard and pointy. Reaching around, I felt its shape. It was a book. Did my Little Shadow like to read?

I wondered what she read about. Pirates and dragons? Boring-ass non-fiction, or a princess getting woken up by a handsome prince?

I laughed at the thought, an image of a ruthless killer with her nose shoved in a book.

How human of her.

Leaving that for now, I ran my hands along the tent floor again, finding some extra clothing. I picked it up, and a light perfume of citrus and jasmine filled my nose. It certainly didn't reek like the vapid females who came to my club. I still couldn't scrub off the latest crap off my dick.

My Little Shadow smelled pleasant—a calming, earthy scent. Intrigued, I dug around further and found a smaller piece of clothing. Putting it to my nose and inhaling, I was surprised to find my cock swelling again. I thought the intricacy with how the shadow handled her prey was what had the appendage kicking before, but now…

The scent on the item was the unmistakably sweet aroma of her pussy. Rubbing my fingertips along the inside, I couldn't stop myself from sliding those fingers into my mouth. A groan escaped my lips, and I had to resist the urge to grind my hips. Never had I tasted such a flowery, sweet center. I was reminded of lilacs or lilies.

Intoxicating.

The fabric in my hand was so small that I imagined how tiny her waist must be under that ugly-ass baggy sweatshirt she always wore, how slender her stomach was, and how lined the ridges of her hips were. I would bet that those worked like a map to that sweet cunt.

My body shivered. Strangely, the bubbling rage I felt earlier was masked somehow with this vibrating heat spreading everywhere. It had me sweating.

"Fuck," I moaned, pushing the panties into my jean's pocket.

I continued my search, looking for a weapon or more of those satin smooth panties, but I couldn't feel anything else. There was a small, itchy, textured pillow and a scratchy blanket, but I didn't give a fuck about any of that.

My cock throbbed. The damn thing wouldn't stop—the pulsing sent painful twinges to my balls. I wasn't going to walk back to my club with a raging hard-on.

This was just ridiculous.

Laying back with my feet hanging out of the small little tent, I unzipped my jeans and freed the unrelenting bastard.

Her perfume was a goddamn drug to me, and the small space made the smell of her a thousand times more powerful. I closed my eyes, wrapped her panties around myself, and started stroking.

I never could get a good look at my Little Shadow. The only glimpses I'd ever managed were short and blurry. Even a few nights before, her image was in the darkness, as opposed to her smile, which was like the sun. I knew she had light blonde hair. The golden, sun-kissed strands reached down to her luscious ass. I imagined how soft they felt and how she'd whimper when I grabbed her locks, wrapping them between my fingers and pulling hard, making her arch her back for me.

Would she be surprised? Would she be disobedient and try to pull away, or would she like it and rock back harder on my cock?

I hoped she disobeyed. I wanted to force her. I wanted to push her pretty pouty lips down on my dick and make her choke on my come again and again. I wanted to feel what she could do and watch her eyes as she brought me closer and closer to my release.

Cry for me, baby.

I really wanted to see her eyes. Were they brown? Green? Blue? I needed to know. I needed to see them water and pour tears down her pale cheeks. I stroked myself harder. The images of her growing more persistent and moving faster. I felt my balls draw up and my chest tightening.

Would she scream to god? No, it wouldn't be god pleasuring her. It would be me. If she dared give another man credit, I'd punish her harder.

How many times would she come? Five? Maybe eight? I'd make sure to make her count out loud each time that tiny pussy clenched my dick. The orgasm ripped from me. My body coiled like a cobra, releasing with a guttural cry of relief, the orgasm ripped from me.

Holy fuck.

Well, that was new. I stared down in shock at my coated hands and her soaked, dark underwear. Grinning and still a bit shaky, I returned my come-drenched present where I'd found it. It would be hilarious to see her later—confusion and anger on her pretty face at what possibly happened in her little shack of a room.

I would make sure to get a nice view.

My kill could wait. It was time to watch the Little Shadow and her emotions. I wanted her steaming. She would already be fuming from relieving her of her kill, so I wanted to see how she responded to having her castle invaded. I would infiltrate every aspect of her life, taking her apart piece by piece.

Sleep well, Little Shadow. Enjoy my gift.

Chapter 7

Ember

After a morning full of disappointment, I headed back to the cove. My anger was chilling my body, that icy feeling steeling me, making my walk back home harder. I got the usual gasps and whispers from the homeless people, and now Randall greeted me with a glare.

Ignoring it all, I arrived back at my tent and froze.

Something feels off.

Searching around, I didn't notice anything out of place.

Did one of the stragglers come into my area?

Frowning, I opened my tent, the feeling of unease increasing. There was a strange scent in the air—an earthy musk. It smelled faint, but it was there—the smell of a man.

What in the ever-loving fuck?

I crouched down, crawling toward the back of my tent. The smell grew as I closed the space around me. Did someone try to rob me? My book was still there, a dark fairy tale retelling of "Beauty and the Beast," and the clothes I threw off before going hunting were there, too.

Unsure, I lay down on my pillow, puzzled at the weird sensation.

Heat arose on my chest and neck. I started to sweat, and I just felt suffocated. I dug into my bag of clothes, stripping off my hoodie and tank top, letting the breeze from the river hit my fevered skin.

The cool air caressed my nipples, and the relief made me sigh in contentment until I found my black thong near the tent's entrance. It was slightly damp, and I tried to recall if I'd gotten caught in the rain or maybe had been sweating from pulling that lanky tweaker from my car.

Feeling that strange heat again, I lifted the garment to my nose. The unmistakable scent of musky salt and chlorine was so strong that I could taste the smell on my tongue.

"Ewwwe," I gasped, dropping the panties to the floor.

What in the sick fuck?

Did one of the homeless men think it would be funny to play a prank on me? Did those ballsy motherfuckers think they could violate my sleeping quarters?

Like hell.

Disgusted, I threw the underwear into the darkness of the tunnel that was about five feet from my tent. The damp thud when it hit the ground made me gag. Pausing to catch my breath, I thought about Randell. I knew he was mad at me, but I never dreamed he'd stoop to a college-level prank.

"Damn," I muttered, rifling in my bag for a different pair.

I didn't keep many clothes here, but I hid bags around the city. That way, wherever I ended up that night, I knew where the closest stash would be. My hand landed on my sequined red cocktail dress, and I paused. Chewing my bottom lip, I knew what this dress meant. I knew where it could lead…

"Oh, fuck it."

I yanked the dress out of the bag and over my body without anything on underneath. This damn thing only went as low as my ass cheeks, and if I so much as sneezed, it was going to give anyone close by a free show.

Well, it looks like it'll be a party.

The noisy club had me stiffening. All these people bumping up against me, some trying to grind on me until my face showed them what a bad idea that was. Finally, finding the bar, I sat down on the first empty stool I touched.

After a while, I started to think this was pointless and that I was wasting my time until a man's arm reached out and grabbed me.

"Sorry about that," a nice, male baritone voice said. Pausing, I grasped onto his arm and squeezed back.

"No problem," I said.

Four big, tall, burly men lined up beside the man who'd just gripped my arm. As they approached the bar, I covertly flanked them, moving so I was sitting only a few seats away.

"Hey, gorgeous." The handsome bartender gave me a blindingly white smile. "What are you having tonight?"

I worried my lip.

I didn't drink because I absolutely didn't want to end up like the alcoholic who birthed me into this fucked up world.

"Uh. A Shirley Temple," I said, trying to speak over the booming music that had my teeth chattering. The bartender looked at me while trying not to laugh. His neatly faded brown-black hair shook with the movement of his head.

"Nah. That's for kids." He was grinning at me. "You need something like a Dirty Russian or a Sex-On-The-Beach?"

I snorted derisively, knowing the truth was that I probably

needed both. He looked at me, and his eyes were kind. I sighed and plastered on a smile to match his.

"Okay," I said. "And a water, please."

I wasn't going to drink the liquor, but if it made this guy happy to give me a cocktail, fine. I'd just dump it on one of the plants when he wasn't looking. I turned my head to hear the men next to me. I couldn't see them clearly because of how their bodies were positioned, but I could hear them just fine, even over the music.

Facing a random person, I started to mouth different song lyrics to look like I was in a conversation if one of the men glanced my way. It probably looked like I was talking to myself, but whatever. I just needed to keep up the illusion.

"Rocky ain't been back for a week now," one of them said, slamming his glass back on the bar.

"You think they got him?" Another said, his voice had a wheezy tone.

"That or the popos got him." The one closest to me agreed.

"I don't know. It's all a bit weird. Rocky was meeting with a newbie from Syracuse. He was supposed to carry our shipment and start up a chain there."

The group contemplated that, their silence stretching for a beat.

"Does the Butcher know about this shit?" the wheezy guy spoke up.

The tallest shadowy figure of the bunch sighed. "Who the fuck knows. I think it's worldwide news at this point that a fucking serial killer is picking us off like flies. They got Dez, too. Saw it on a damn newspaper."

Wheezy gasped. "No shit? Well, hell, we need to find this Snow White bitch and repay them for what they've been doing to our crew."

"I ain't looking for no serial killer, Ed."

"Shut the fuck up, both of you dumbasses." The gruff voice guy, who seemed to be the leader, clapped a meaty hand on the bar. "We're not gonna look for that psycho, but we ain't gonna let them keep mowing us down either."

I smirked, pretending to drink my water.

"Yeah, boss, that's smart." His wheezy breath was unsettling as he agreed.

A new voice spoke up. "I think the best thing we can do is lay low. Slow the supplies for a bit or relocate outside of Roch."

I blinked. This guy wasn't an idiot. His crew would be wise to listen.

"You're afraid of a storybook princess, but you're gonna know fear when the Butcher gets you for talking like that," the smart guy said.

"Not to mention the Ripper," another said, a shiver in his voice.

I knew of the Butcher, but this Ripper character...I would need to do more investigating.

I felt a heat on the back of my neck and whipped around to find a man in the corner. His head was down, but his eyes were focused on me through his black wavy hair.

I glared back. I didn't need some pervert staring at me. More than likely, plenty of girls would jump at the opportunity to be with this guy. His fancy suit and that dark midnight hair with thick curly waves falling into his face announced danger like a neon sign.

"Meet me out in the alley, boys. We need to have a meeting." The guy, who I now would guess to be the leader, got up and walked in the direction where I knew a side door to the alley sat.

I decided to ignore the leering 'neon sign' for now and followed after the guys at the bar.

Stepping outside the door, still feeling the vibration of the thumping music, I walked forward, only to feel myself being lifted off the ground, my shoulders pinched in a bruising grip.

"Well, well, well, boys." The leader laughed, and I could feel his eyes studying me while my heels fell off my feet, clacking to the ground with a pathetic *click*. "Looks like we have ourselves a shiny new toy," he continued, showing me off to his friends.

My dress was riding up, and I knew my bare ass was exposed now. Anger engulfed me, and its burn awakened every muscle in my body.

"Oh, what a sweet ass," the wheezy guy crooned, a stinging smack landing on my bare bottom.

I glared, letting the ice complete its seize over me.

The small pocket on my dress was reachable. I only needed to distract these buffoons.

"Put me down, and I'll give you a show," I offered, trying to purr as best I could.

I watched their eyes in the dim light, and every pair of eyes ogling me shouted 'violence.'

Good. 'Cause I was ready to play.

The meathead boss placed me on my feet. Stepping back a small step, I used my feet to find my shoes and leaned over, ensuring my bare ass was on full display. The men hooted and groaned.

I gagged in my mouth and grabbed my shoes. With two quick snaps, I broke off the heels of my stilettos.

Spinning around to face the men, I ran at the two smaller guys, embedding my heels in their necks. Blood leaked from their wounds and their mouths as they went down in unison.

The other two men fumbled with their unlatched belts when I leaned down to grab my shoes, trying to recover from the shock of what had just happened. Holding their arms out to shield themselves almost made me chuckle. I grabbed my needle from my pocket and reached for the wheezy guy. Grabbing his shirt, I slammed the metal into his chest.

"You bitch!" Wheezy coughed, his breaths coming out even more with that awful hiss.

The last man, the boss, ran at me like a bull, roaring in rage at his comrades' death. Feeling the air shift, I knew where he was and sidestepped him. A low growl sounded from behind me as I spun on my heel.

This was gonna hurt.

The leader tackled me like a fully suited-up defensive lineman. Accepting the dizzying *crack* on my head, I hit the ground and felt the hilt of something shoving into my side. Reaching down, I snagged it. It was a knife.

Perfect timing…

Turning it around, I waited for him to slam down again on top of me. His knife was pointed up, and I slammed it into his chest as he fell. His immediate gargling gasp filled the night air as he flipped over.

"Y-you?" he managed, his mouth filling with blood as the haunting realization of his death hit him.

I smiled and stood up. Stepping by his head, I looked down at him, wanting to see his remaining breaths. His mouth and chest were painted entirely with blood—the perfect color of red.

"Yep. It's me. Enjoy your eternal slumber. Another justice awarded, another life saved, another death avenged." I blew him a kiss, watching as he flinched. The full understanding finally clicked in his brain.

"Snow Whi-White."

I hated that stupid name. Cops were too blasé. Naming me after a fairytale princess gave the wrong impression to young girls. Then again, maybe not. The Grimm brothers sure told the tale in its true glory. I certainly didn't think the animated version was much better than me. They murdered parents in front of children, for crying out loud. At least I killed the bad guys.

At this moment, I was more like Cinder with no 'Ella' added. My poor shoes were ruined, and I realized my dress was too.

Very well, I guess I'm wearing flats.

Ducking back into the club, I ran to the bathroom, where I found a random girl passed out in the corner.

Thank you, Fairy Overseerer….

Also, it was convenient as hell because I didn't feel like cleaning blood off my dress. I stripped her out of her gown and pulled it up my body. It was a dingy yellow color, and it clashed with my hair.

Sighing, I shook my head, pulled myself together, and walked out.

To my surprise, the man from that corner was outside the door. His face was lit up by the overhead lights that were stationed by the bathrooms. Up close, I could make out his features better. He was fucking gorgeous. Every bit the heartbreaker rich boy, his nice gray tailored suit, suggested.

"I liked you better in red," he stated. His lazy tone confirmed my playboy suspicions. He leaned against the wall, staring at me and twirling a card in his hand.

I narrowed my eyes at him.

He was paying too much attention to me.

"I don't remember asking your opinion." I glared at his light green eyes. Damn, they looked like cut emeralds when I was close enough to really see them.

He shrugged indifferently. With one long, heated gaze, his eyes drifted down my body. Then he wandered off back to the bar. Happy he got the hint, I waited and paced around a bit more while chatting to random people I didn't give a shit about to create an alibi if this led to police sniffing around the cove again. I had heard they were there, and it pissed me off to have them rifling around like they cared at all about the people living there.

After I was satisfied with the number of people who spotted me in this ugly yellow dress, I walked back into that dark alley next to the bar. I wrapped an oversized jacket around my body that I'd stolen from a random hook inside and went to find the man I'd knocked out earlier. Slowly, I dragged him out from behind the garbage cans I'd left him behind. He was still out cold from the drug cocktail I'd given him.

Time to find out who this Ripper was.

Chapter 8

*H*ere we were up at the crack of dawn. Again. This shit had to stop. Based on Quinn's face, it was clear that he was feeling the same way. We yawned in unison. My body ached, and my migraine was constantly a dull throb in my head.

"Looks like we need to be at the club on Beverly," Quinn said, handing me a laptop. The thing looked strange to be owned by Quinn. It was pink with glittery stickers all over it.

Maybe it was his late sister's?

I opened it up, Googling the club and reading the first article that pulled up. A gorgeous black, wavy-haired guy was smiling at the cameras. He wore an expensive-looking baby blue suit, his lazy grin looking like he could melt the panties off of anyone. Ugh, he irked me. There was something about his light green eyes that just made me mad.

"What does it say about the owner?" Quinn said, pulling over on Clay Street. We weren't far from the scene now.

"Besides him looking like a devilish playboy?" I snorted, brushing off the feeling of lust that tangled in my gut and heated my body. "His name is Lucius 'vas-il-ee-iv. Vasiliev? An arrogant fuck head with too much money and some supermodel on his arm."

Quinn had a smile playing on his lips, a humorous interest in those baby blues of his. "Anything about the club? The man being clearly Russian, I wonder if he has any affiliation with Moya Kotova."

I gaped at him.

The Russian mafia? No way. This guy wasn't Bratva. Was he?

"I don't know why I'm being dragged along for this. I'm supposed to be dealing solely with Snow White. The chief keeps making me do his work because he's too damn lazy."

I cringed at my own words, realizing I let my anger get the best of me. That was stupid to say with such a by-the-book-order-following soldier like Quinn.

His booming, husky laugh made me visibly jump. It was the last thing I expected to hear. "Isn't that the truth?" he said through his musical laughter. I stared at my partner like he was an alien, waiting for him to chastise or scold me for being childish. "At any rate," he continued. "I'm glad you're on the case. If I get stuck with Emily one more time, I am going to lose my shit."

Now, I was the one laughing.

Emily must have really stepped in it with their last investigation. I'd heard they went on a stakeout with their confidential informant. However, they got some information about the Butcher, so that was good. If we could find this man before Snow White did, we'd finally have the upper hand.

Arriving at the scene, I was starting to want to give this killer a high five, not a prison sentence. There was no real connection to Snow White, so it looked like another crime of passion. Three guys were laid out by a dumpster in the back alley behind the club.

Thin heels were impaling the necks of two victims, and the last one lost in a knife fight. He was gripping the knife that was now sunk into his fat gut. Ally walked up to me. Her horn-rimmed glasses made her eyes wide. She pointed to a random spot more toward the back, a few feet from the other dead bodies.

Her coffin-black nails sparkled in the sun. Her lacey purple gloves made her look like the eighties gothic queen she was.

"So, I could be wrong, Ella, but I think Chief Doger wanted you here because this may be your Princess killer after all."

My eyes grew wide, waiting for her to continue. She pulled me along the alley by the back end and pointed to the ground, where there was a weird pattern of blood.

"This blood splatter around this area here...." She pointed to the circular dark wall. "And here." She pointed to an area with a puddle of clear liquid that looked to have dried up. "It makes me think there was another person with these guys, and our killer took the individual."

She pushed her black glasses up, and her deep brown eyes looked calculated as she walked to the far back wall of the area.

"I also deduce that there was a car parked here. This liquid was from an air conditioner." She gestured to the faint stain on the pavement. "My guess is Snow White killed these other ogres, and whoever the other person was took the one they could better manage."

"Agreed," I said.

Ally smiled, and her slightly downturned eyes gleamed with pride.

"That's what I thought too, El. The blood splatter near the other guys shows a distinct pattern shadowed out. It's smaller in frame and height than the others. My guess is our unsub took him to question him further instead of killing him here with his goons. The blood that was there has to be his comrades."

Watching everything unfold before my eyes, I let my imagination create the full picture. "Did anyone see our unsub in the club?"

Ally scrunched her nose. "Well sure, probably, but there are two issues with that. A: We don't know if the other person is a girl or a smaller guy. B: We checked the CCTV footage in the club, and it's so dark in there with so many people bouncing around that Quinn said he couldn't see shit. Doger is pissed. He keeps asking for club access to talk to the owner, but that guy won't give us permission. His burly bodyguards won't even let anyone talk to him face to face."

I frowned. Of course, that pretty boy wouldn't want to be bothered by the police. His business was probably shady as hell. Quinn walked up to us, his brow drawn, and his lips looked more pink than usual, suggesting he may have been chewing on them.

What had him so ruffled?

"So what did we figure out, ladies?" he said, masking his lapse in demeanor. I didn't even think Ally noticed.

"Well, Miss Ally Wu is a freaking genius," I said, watching her puff up like a peacock at my praise. "She followed a blood pattern to the back alley and saw that it didn't add up. We're missing a victim, and we're missing a car from the scene."

Quinn clapped a congratulatory pat on Ally's shoulder. She was so short that he had to bend down. It made me giggle to myself watching the action. "Nice work, Wu."

Ally had the biggest crush on Quinn, and I had to root for her, watching her blush. My phone buzzed, and I used it as an excuse to leave the two of them alone. Ally began recapping her genius to Quinn, who was smiling and watching her with interest.

"This is Ella," I answered, standing by the frame of the door to the alley.

"Smella! I need you to meet me at the bar tonight. A client gave me big news about the dealer you're trying to catch—Chopper or something like that."

I gasped, lowering my voice and covering the mouthpiece with my palm.

"The Butcher? Cassie, how?" She seemed to be fidgeting. I could hear her shuffling her feet nervously and instantly became worried. "Cass, what's going on? How did you get this information?"

I heard a slight pause, and then she sighed, frustration clear in her usually chipper tone. "It doesn't matter how Ella. I have it, and if you want it, you'll meet me at the bar tonight at eight."

My stomach dropped, a feeling of dread lacing inside my throat, choking me.

Steadying my breath, I walked back over to the group. Quinn immediately noticed my expression and moved toward me with a worried look on his face.

"Ella? You okay?"

He had such a big brother way of speaking to me. I couldn't help but want to tell him everything, but I couldn't. For Cassie's safety, I had to keep my mouth shut.

"Oh, nothing. I guess I just ate something weird." Forcing a laugh, I waved away their stares. "So, I'm going to try and get the club douche to talk to us," I said, not waiting around to be pestered again. I walked around the alley to the front, where big purple and gold doors awaited me.

Jesus, this guy loved to flaunt his wealth.

I braced myself, knocking on the massive entrance. The purple front covering the door felt like furniture that you might find in a 50s-style diner.

The door opened, and I tried to peer inside but was blocked by two humongous bodyguards. They were the tallest men I'd ever seen. One looked like a Samoan king, and the other looked just as much the bodybuilder sort. His beautiful dark skin only accentuated his solid build.

"Uh…" I stammered, astonished by the instant fear I had

swirling around in my gut. I had to raise my head so far up just to look at the bottom of their chin.

Neither bothered looking down at me. They just stood like statues, their arms crossed and their bodies unmovable.

"Club hours are 9:00 pm to 2:00 am," one said, still not bothering to glance at me.

"Well, I am not here for that. I need to speak to the owner of this establishment. My name is Ella Fox. I am a criminal analyst with the Rochester Police Department."

Finally, the Samoan man slid his eyes down to stare at me. He turned his head, giving his partner a look with his eyes—a message, but one I couldn't decipher.

The man with beautiful dark skin looked down now, too. My eyes squinted in the glaring sun to meet his glare.

"Mr. Vasiliev does not communicate with law enforcement," he stated.

His voice was more of a rumble than a tone. It made the hairs on my skin stand up. Of course, this asshead wouldn't talk to cops.

"Well, if Mr. Vasiliev doesn't want to be seen as interfering with an open investigation of a homicide, I suggest he learn to gain some manners." I scowled up at the stone-like men. They exchanged another look and shut the indigo-lined door in my face.

The bar at *Jay's* was homey as usual. The 1920s theme gave the entire place a fun atmosphere, but for once, the oldie's music and classically dressed rollerblading servers couldn't cure my sour mood.

I tapped my foot on the metal rung under the old school table as the minutes ticked by—Cassie was late, and my heartbeat picked up with each passing second.

"Where the hell are you, Cassie?" I whispered to myself.

"Hiya, doll. What can I grab for you this fine night?" The chipper tone of the young waitress was like a slap to my ears.

I jolted, looking up at her smiling face and classically done 1920s thick black eyelashes, pretty pink blush, and the notorious ruby red lipstick.

"Uh, just a water for now," I mumbled, looking around her at the door for the umpteenth time.

Deciding my patience was too thin, I dialed her number and brought the receiver to my ear. It went straight to voicemail.

Again.

Trying not to shake visibly, I left a clipped message asking 'where in the ever-loving fuck she was' and hung up. My nerves were shot, and my nails were bleeding stubs. Glancing up, I caught a glimpse of a figure in the doorway.

My sister.

She was safe.

Standing up, I ran over to her and squeezed the living daylights out of her. "Oh my god! Cassandra Eva Fox, I am going to kill you!"

She squeaked from my rough hug and tapped my shoulders where she could reach.

"Ella, you know I love my dieting, but you're about to make me puke up my lunch," she said in a breathless tone.

I let her go and stared at her.

She was in a black knee-length dress. Her short brown hair was perfectly curled, her makeup flawless, and her signature platform heels, which had black lace on the front of them and an intricate design on the side of them, covered her feet.

"You had me worried sick," I said, wagging my finger at her.

She grinned sheepishly. "Sorry, my client ran late."

I gave her a pointed look. My aggravation was evident. "I'm

going to chop off this client's dick. I thought something happened to you."

She sighed. The exasperation and tiredness started to crack her perfect mask.

"I'm sorry," she said again more sincerely. "I got here as soon as I could. My phone died because I was on the outskirts of town, and I lost my charger between the couch cushions or something yesterday."

I blinked, rolling my eyes, but accepted her answer.

Sitting down, I calmed my breathing and finally spoke up. "So, what is this information?" Lowering my tone, I leaned forward. "About the Butcher? And how did you get it?"

She grinned triumphally with sparkles in her blue-gray eyes.

"Well…" she said primly. "I slept with him."

I gaped at her, waiting for a 'gotchya' to come with that statement, but it didn't. "You did what?"

My body physically began shutting down, but she continued. "Yeah. So, Margo told me a big baddie wanted something new, and I asked her to set up a meet."

I couldn't form words, and she took that as a sign to continue.

"It wasn't long. He is like the quickest fuck I've ever had. He paid a few grand and gave me his card with the name of some warehouse in West Stanton."

I snatched the card from her manicured hands, staring at the name and trying to run through where the fuck that could be.

"I don't understand," I said, sounding stupid.

She smiled brightly, her pearly white teeth gleaming. "I wanted to help you, Ella. And I did. I found your big bad guy. After my flake of a boyfriend ran off, I wanted to be useful."

My heart squeezed, and my fear spiked. My poor sister just got in a literal bed with the devil. Why? All so she could help me because I was too incompetent to find the idiot myself.

I wanted to throw up.

"Oh, and guess what? He has a friend named Pedro. And I gave him my ticket for the art gala tomorrow."

I continued to stare at her. My mouth and tongue were not able to function. The art gala was directly adjacent to *Black Mirrors*. The club had just had a triple homicide in the alley next to it, and it was possibly connected to a kidnapping and my serial killer.

Cassie just set me up on a date, and not just any date, but with a known drug cartel leader's partner and possibly a part of the largest Russian mafia.

Moya Kotova…My blood.

I wondered just how much of my blood was going to be shed in this crazy plan or if I would even come out alive.

Chapter 9

Ember

Stretching out of my curled-up position on the park bench, I checked my phone. It was a little past three in the morning.

Damn.

Those meth slingers from the club the other night had a fair amount of cash on them, and their bank accounts were plentiful. I was happy to clean them out.

Got a good forty-grand, so I was able to acquire some needed essentials for everyone in the camp.

I made my way back to the cove, ensuring my hoodie was pulled over my hair. The homeless community was fast asleep, so I tried to tiptoe back to the docks as quietly as possible. At each of the twenty-four cart areas where their other things were stored, I dropped a bag of goodies as soundlessly as I could at each spot. They were full of water canteens, battery-operated stove tops, reinforced netting tents, and a multitude of foods. Plus, there was an envelope of a thousand dollars for each dwelling.

After delivering my last bag, I paused to scan the area. The dock was comforting as usual, the humid salty air clinging to my hair and skin. The seasons were changing from frigid cold to a sweet springtime. Rochester was infamous for having fifty-four-degree weather one day and a blizzard the next, though, so just because it was spring technically didn't mean much.

The breeze from the river picked up a sour smell, and my nose scrunched up in distaste. I peered at the river, leaning over, expecting to see the wheezy man floating on the river's top. But no, he was fish chow by now, and I didn't see anything resembling that I'd made a mistake in his demise.

Still, the air continued to sour with that metallic scent that could only be blood. I furrowed my brows, looking over to the tunnel that was never used. The thing was pitch black, and the only thing in it was stairs leading out of a maintenance hole to the city.

As I walked toward the dark space, the smell intensified.

Did an animal wander in here and die?

The iron smell was insanely strong, making the entire tunnel a perfumed box of rot.

Walking deeper in, trailing my hands on the rusted, rough, textured walls, I felt something wet at my feet. It could be rain from the cracks in the overhead bridge or a pool of blood-based on the smell.

The tunnel was the darkest part of the docks. It was always a dimly lit place, but there was usually enough light for me to make out my surroundings. But at the moment, I couldn't see my own hand in front of my face.

I strained my ears to listen for any noise.

The roar of the highway above and the distant water dripping echoed around the space, but I couldn't detect anything else.

Crouching down, I ran my fingers along the pool, seeking the disturbance in the energy of the air. There was a heat to the area, my breaths bouncing back to me as they collided with whatever the object in front of me was.

Finding purchase on what felt like a human foot, I kept trailing my hand up.

First, my fingertips hit large breasts with a sticky pool in the center, and the fabric, soaking in what could only be blood, spilled over with my touch. Finally, I found the neck of the female had been sliced, a gash opening from ear to ear.

I glared into the darkness.

Who the fuck killed this woman?

And why was her body left next to my home?

Anger boiled in my blood. Maybe there was another drug mule I had missed at the club. Perhaps someone had arrived late and saw me dispatch their friends. I sighed at the irritation of what having a body on my turf brought. I'd just dealt with the brainless runt dealer earlier, and now I had this, too. It took hours to scrub blood off any surface. Grumbling, I grabbed the woman's arms and pulled her back toward my tent.

When the dim light hit her face, I instantly recognized her. She was a hooker from Child Street. I often dealt in sex work to get the girls' intel and keep up on the fresh players. Most of the time, clients ended up dead mysteriously before they got anything out of me, and I wasn't exactly known for being the most docile collaborator.

This girl's name was Tanisha. She was a nice enough girl. Older than some of the others but not wanted as much by the clients. Still, it was a shame that she was killed. She wasn't bad, just unwanted. I walked over to the dock and grabbed the bucket and scrub brush. Walking back over, I noticed a small object in her hand. Picking it out of her grip, I stared at an origami apple.

Mother. Fucker.

I needed to find this paper-folding stalker, who apparently had an affinity for knife work. I leaned down, staring more intently at the wound, the lines jagged—a pattern my dagger used to leave in my victims.

God, my back ached from earlier. Cleaning the vomit and snot off of the sniveling loser drug dealer was no easy task. Now, I had to clean up blood from a cheeky maniac.

With all my anger and frustration, I navigated back to the tunnel and began scrubbing at the pools of liquid. I doused the area in sudsy water and bleach and listened as it washed through the cracks in the foundation, dropping into the river below the concrete.

This asshole was trying to frame me.

I knew from the minute I heard cops were sniffing around the cove that I was being framed. I never left loose ends. Ever. I did my job and cleaned up like a good girl or at least left the low life in their own home or a random abandoned one so I could skip that annoying step. *Who the fuck wanted to be a housekeeper?*

I lived in a tent in an abandoned dock for a reason. Hell, I wanted to hire a maid for even my tent space, but something told me it would be frowned upon to ask a cleaning service to scrub up a hitman's blood.

Finally satisfied with the tangy iron smell dissipating and being replaced by an eye-watering chemical smell, I walked back to finish taking care of the fallen hooker. Saying a quick little vigil for her and her family, I tied the rocks around her ankles, strapped a spare bag with a bowling ball in it to her back, and shoved her into the river's dark depths.

Stalking back to the club, I knocked on the massive purple doors. The moose and bear gang stared at me with unreadable expressions.

"Let me in, losers. It's midnight, and you're clearly open."

Exchanging another look, one man started to say something, but then that man, the playboy from last night, shoved the one guy aside, ushering me in with a devilish grin playing at the corners of his lips.

"Ah, malen' kaya ten'. Welcome back."

Nodding, I hid my smile. For some reason, knowing he called me 'little one' made me…I dunno, but whatever. Shaking that feeling off, I looked around at the club because I had work to do. The booming music that vibrated my bones before was now gone, replaced by a soft, jazzy beat. There wasn't anyone in the large space either, no grinding, sweaty dancers, sweet-talking bartenders, or robotic guards lining the entryways.

Nothing.

Just this strange man.

And me.

Unease and suspicion heated my chest.

Stopping near the bar, I turned to look in the corner where the overhead lights illuminated the bathrooms. I had left that dress from the other night in there. I'd stashed it inside the toilet's ceramic lid in the last stall.

I had come to retrieve it, taking any of my DNA with it. Choosing to ignore the fact that this place was deserted, I shoved my unease away.

"I just came to use your bathroom," I said to the playboy.

The tall, dark-haired man smiled, a playful mirth swirling in his mesmerizing green orbs. "But of course, right over that way."

He gestured, and I had a strange sense of doubt. Still, I ducked around him and charged for the bathroom, catching his broody reflection in the multitude of mirrors in his fun-house horror game as he watched my every step.

Feeling my way to the stall and ripping off the top of the toilet, I cursed when I found nothing nestled in the clean, clear waters.

Panicked, I looked around, checking the back of each toilet in all six stalls.

"What the fuck?" I began pacing around and biting my nails.

Did that man know about the dress? Did cleaners find it and throw it out? Did the police come and take it?

I checked my phone, scrolling over the article about an alley massacre, but there was no mention of a woman or any evidence found inside the club. I balked at a paragraph that caught my eye. The club owner, Lucius Vasiliev, the owner of *Black Mirrors*, was stated to have refused any statement regarding the investigation, and a warrant for the club was now pending. This state of affairs would force the club doors shut until the situation was handled.

That icy chill ran down my spine again. So, the ghost was the owner.

I walked out the bathroom doors, mumbling on my way through the door frame. "Lucius."

"I do love my name on a beautiful woman's lips."

I jumped at the intrusion. The devil himself was lazily perched on the bartop, eyeing me curiously.

Not wanting to engage, I put my hands on my hips. "I lost something. Do you know where it is?"

He hopped off the bar table and walked over to me, his smile widening into a deep chasm. His pale green eyes flickered with sardonic joy. He was close to me, his heat a vibration on my skin.

Suddenly, I felt like a mouse about to be pounced on by a cruel cat. Not for any other reason but to enjoy his own sick satisfaction of playing a game and making his prey suffer.

"Are you referring to this, Little Shadow?" he purred in his husky rasp, walking over and pulling my red dress from behind his bar, the blood stains shining in the overhead light.

I swallowed, searching his face for exactly what game he was playing.

"Or, perhaps this?"

I audibly gasped when my dagger came into sight. My dad's intricately carved crown reflected light on this beautiful monster's face.

"The police wanted these so badly," he continued, frowning and weighing my dagger in his hand, gently twirling the sharp blade expertly through his fingers. "But alas, I don't like to give up my treasures."

I grimaced at him.

"Those aren't yours," I argued, stepping closer but keeping my body stance toward the exit door. "They are mine."

"Finders keepers and all that." He tsked at me, shaking his head and letting those inky black waves fall into his eyes. "You'd think a pretty princess would be more careful with her toys, no?"

I narrowed my eyes, advancing slowly. He chuckled, his shoulders rising with a smug expression playing on his features.

"You should take care of what's yours." I ignored him, but he continued anyway. "I guess even the best of us make mistakes."

He twirled around the table, evading my silent advances.

"Isn't that right?" Pausing, he captured my face in his hands and purred near my ear. "Snow White."

I stopped, not even to breathe, as I turned my head to stare at him in stunned silence. How did he know I was the serial killer? Did he see me kill those men? No, he didn't, and I hadn't used my usual MO. I was careful to make it appear as a self-defense kill. He had to know about my identity some other way.

He chuckled at me again, surely watching the gears turn in my head. He twirled the dagger so intricately and expertly in his hands that the sliced prostitute in the tunnel by my home clouded my mind. The jagged cut had the identical shape of my blade.

"Look, Little Shadow, I don't need sharp objects in my possession, so I'm willing to make you a deal."

I stiffened, standing in place. He practically danced on his toes as he yawned and straightened his white tie.

Growing annoyed, I took the bait. "What?"

He smiled wider now, walking back to the bar's table, gesturing for me to sit across from him on what looked like a couch. His reflection bounced in the mirrors with each step he took. I watched his movements as I walked down the aisle and sat at the place facing him on a pristinely white sofa.

"You can have your precious dagger back." He started dancing toward me. "But not before I watch you use it."

I grinned now, happy to slice this fool into ribbons.

"On your sweet little cunt…" He licked the handle and then used it to edge up the hem of my dress.

I slapped it back down, shoving at him with a curse. He chuckled and simply watched me. He was holding the dagger out, the sharp tip in his grip, the glistening handle jutting toward me.

"You seriously think I'm going to fuck myself with my own knife?" I spat, ready to get up.

He didn't flinch. Instead, he grabbed his phone and flipped to an image that made me pale. Randall was sitting beside an elderly homeless man. His smile was radiant as he helped him open the package I had left, and tears of happiness streamed down both their faces when they looked around and saw all the others opening their gifts.

"You're a generous little princess to your dwarves, aren't you?" he mocked, running his hand over my cheek and tucking a stray hair behind my ear.

I ground my teeth together, feeling like they would surely shatter.

"I could always do it for you," he offered, his raspy tone sending chills down my spine as he whispered them in my ear.

He was watching me, watching my people and my friends. I started to put the pieces together and realized this man was my stalker. The one who left dead bodies for me to clean up and fucking paper apples littered around my home.

"Did you jack off in my underwear, you creep?" I said, putting the puzzle pieces together too.

He gave me a wicked grin. His eyes glittered with approval at my knowledge of the full picture.

"I tasted you, Little Shadow. You taste so sweet and warm. I must admit I'm not used to wanting someone so much, and I hate you. You've been the bane of my existence for a while now. Stalling my operations and taking down big numbers that I have in my control."

I studied him, trying to find a lie in his words.

He was telling the truth. Which meant he would kill Randall if I didn't satisfy his sick fantasy.

"Why not kill me now then?" I challenged, snatching the dagger from him at last.

He laughed this time, a genuine musical sound.

"Silly girl. We both know that would lead the police right to my door. I'm not going to make things easy for you."

I cursed under my breath. Clearly, he wasn't going to come close enough for me to take him down.

The image of Randall and the homeless people so happy with their gifts flashed in my mind. I sighed, and with a glare filled with all my hate and ice, I met Lucius Vasiliev's gaze, making sure he could see me in all of his mirrors as I lifted up my dress and pushed the handle of my blade into my core.

Chapter 10

Lucius

Seeing my Little Shadow gasp at her unexpected pleasure had my cock swelling in my pants. A surprising but visceral growl escaped from my lips. I was enraptured, watching the handle slide back and forth inside her tight little pussy. Her anger was swirling in her eyes, like flecks of concrete cracking in the irises.

Beautiful.

I moved closer to her, my movements steady and slow, assuring she didn't startle.

"You're a psychopath." She followed each of my steps with those eyes, her breathing picking up and her hand stilling just slightly.

Offering her a shit-eating grin, I returned, "Awe, thank you, baby, but I prefer creative."

The dreamy glaze in her eyes started to sober, and her sounds turned robotic. I locked my eyes onto hers, grabbing the knife's sharp belly and feeling the slice in my palm as she halted completely. The handle was halfway inside her. The inner edge glistened with her wetness.

"That's not how this is going to work, moya malen' kaya ten'," I growled. "If you don't make that little cunt weep…the deal is off.

You'll leave here with nothing but uncertainty about when I will strike your little castle."

Her silence felt heated, though her body was as still as stone.

"Now," I said, my tone calmer, silky, charged. "You're going to let yourself feel this."

I tested the handle, slowly pushing the blade into her sex—a breath's distance from her quivering chest. My need grew with each beat of her heart, to kiss her, to feel those soft lips on mine...I wondered if they felt as soft as her skin.

Does her tongue taste as sweet as her core?

"Fine," she whimpered, knocking me from my thoughts.

Her breathing was coming out in little pants. I could feel it on my face, tickling my lips and blowing my hair away from my eyes.

Fuck.

"Do I need to *show* you how to please that little pussy of yours?"

"No," she whispered, but her body was writhing, sweat dripping down her neck from straining.

But she did not attempt to push me off.

I nudged the handle deeper.

The blade sliced my palm, and my blood dripped down onto her thighs. Her eyes rolled to the back of her head. Hiding those captivating, beautiful eyes from me....

"Don't you fucking dare," I warned, increasing my speed and dipping the blade upward so that the very top of the blade teased her clit.

She gasped, her moan sharp, almost like a cry. Her eyes were staring into mine now.

She gripped my suit jacket lapels and twisted so the material frayed. I turned my head, watching her pale hand grip the tattered fabric.

She'd done that on purpose.

So, she wanted to play, did she? Very well.

Her sounds of pleasure increased in volume, echoing. They were like a song to my ears. I watched those pouty lips in every single one of the mirrors surrounding us. My cock was so strangled behind my slacks that it had become painful, but I was not going to break my gaze from hers for even a second.

"Fuck," she cried, twisting the fabric more. "You."

A piece of my jacket finally tore free into her grasp. That dangerous little hand of hers latched onto my pectorals, the sting of her nails slicing into my skin and sending a warm heat down my body. The handle of her knife was no longer visible. The entirety of it sunk deep in her warm center.

My hand was drenched, the handle becoming increasingly slippery as I fucked her deep and hard with its length.

I'd never wanted to be a goddamn weapon more than I did right now.

My kills were all made with my own body. I never needed anything to end a life—just my hands. Now, I couldn't shake the image of sinking balls deep inside this goddess and her coating me with that sweet liquid.

"I hate you," she panted, her body pink with a hot blush, her chest rising and falling, her whimpers increasing in volume and tempo.

Fuck.

All too aware of the head of my cock, I felt precome soiling my trousers.

The irony was that I had intended to ruin her dress, yet here I was, with my clothes destroyed. She'd shredded my jacket and now was working on my button-up shirt. The buttons popped and flew off in all directions. The soft tinkling sound they made on the tile as they bounced was sexy.

"Fucking hate me, Kayate," I urged, her thighs slippery with her juices and my blood.

She was rocking back and forth on the edge of the knife bend, letting it rub her clit and glide her slick heat on my hand.

"Fuck."

Rock.

"You."

Grind.

"Lucius."

At the sound of my name, her orgasm ripped through her. Her body shaking and convulsing like a woman possessed. I couldn't look away from her, my own orgasm taking hold. My cock was a battering ram that refused to soften and instead simply twitched with the need to claim her.

The final waves of pleasure ebbed, and I felt like I'd been hit with an anvil. Exhaustion was stealing my breath. I finally moved my hand, pulling the handle from the sea of come on the couch, and I chuckled.

I felt like a schoolboy watching porn for the first time, but I couldn't seem to stop smiling like an idiot. Her breathing was becoming even, her color losing that orgasmic blush and returning to her soft, creamy vanilla. My blood was smeared all over her thighs and pussy. There was even a small little pool on the couch mingled with her come.

Such a glorious sight...

The sting of the wound on my hand was starting to register slightly, so I turned my hand to look at the slice on my palm, an angry red gash from one side to the other. The blood was making my tattoo of my family insignia blurred. Moya Kotova—how accurate in this moment.

I walked over to the bar, grabbing a towel and a bottle of vodka to dull the sting.

When I started to make my way back, I was only mildly surprised to find just the remnants of our pleasure and golden threads from my clothes made by my Little Shadow. Turning just in time, I watched the back of her as she dashed out the door, the dress in hand.

I tipped back the bottle, the heated haze flowing through me, warming my body and fading the sting.

My guard came to the bar, a look of dumbfounded incredulity marking his features.

"The female fled Mr. Vasiliev," he stated, clearing his throat when I didn't respond but instead sighed wistfully.

I did not take my eyes off the beautiful wet mess on the couch across from me. Her scent was on me, mixed with the tang in the air of blood, pleasure, and pain.

Exactly what this girl has brought me.

"Sir?" He stared at me, and the smile I couldn't seem to wipe off my face. "Are you going after her?"

I pondered that for a minute, already knowing I wasn't but wondering why the fuck not.

I waved my hand at my loyal friend, yawning as the drowsiness took control of me.

"No," I said, propping my head back against the wall and closing my eyes. "She'll be back."

Before sleep could wrap its claws fully around me, I gripped the slick dagger, pulling it to my heart. "She's tasted the forbidden fruit, and now she'll need more."

Chapter 11

Ella

Mitzi and Shadow were running around like idiots while I tried to find the perfect outfit for the date with a murdering madman. I sighed, throwing yet another pantsuit behind me onto the floor.

Ugh.

What to wear on a date with a killer?

My phone vibrated on the bed, and I growled, leaning over and pressing the answer button with my toe.

"Cassie, I think I really am going to murder you," I complained, holding up a red camisole and blue jeans to my frame in the mirror across from me.

Maybe not wearing heels is easier, or I could pull a Snow White by using them as a weapon if needed.

Cassie tried to hide her tittering on the other end, and I cursed in protest.

"Yeah, okay! Well, that's a hell of a thank you, Smella," she griped. "Did you take a shower, at least? You don't want to smell like dead people tonight, Babe."

I laughed, not realizing she was serious. When she was just silent, I scoffed in exasperation. "Yes Cass! I am squeaky clean."

"Good!" She squealed, and then my phone lit up on the bed with her pretty face popping up on the screen.

Rolling my eyes but accepting the video chat request, I immediately pointed the phone toward my wardrobe.

"Oh geez, Ella!" she said in a truly horrified tone. "O. M. G. No. I'll be there in ten minutes."

I pressed my lips in a firm line, not knowing what I should have expected from my debutant sister. Twenty minutes later, not ten as she'd promised, my sister smashed through my door with a scowl plastered on her face.

"This. Will. Not. Do," she squawked. She was such a drama queen.

Sighing, I decided to let Cassie just demolish my small closet. It would be better than trying to interfere.

"Ella, you nun," she chastised me while shimmering out of her knee-length dress and tossing it at me. Cassie was taller than me. She was five feet, ten inches, without her platform heels she was always sporting.

I'm only five feet, four inches, and this dress looked longer on me, hugging in weird places. Cassie was supermodel skinny, and I had curves for days, an hourglass figure. So, my ass took up a huge portion of the dress.

Cassie studied me, her face going through a series of different expressions, from perplexed to absolute distaste. Cassie reached up in her hair, pulling out a pin and letting her brown, curly hair cascade down to her shoulders while she yanked me by the bodice to her. She clipped the pin between my breasts and studied me again.

After a minute, she clapped her hands and bounced up and down excitedly.

"Ooooh, I'm a fucking magician," she preened, shoving my ass toward the mirror on the back of my bathroom door.

I had to admit that I did look a lot better than I could have managed.

With her smile wide, she grabbed her old-school Polaroid camera and squeezed me around the shoulders. Her grin was that of a devil. I looked at her, and her genuine happiness allowed me to smile for real as the *click* blinded us.

The photo spat out from the bottom of the camera, and she blew on it while walking into my bathroom and fanning the little portrait until the image showed me and my sister clear as day. Happy, vibrant, and alive. A moment in time captured of true happiness shining in our matching blue-gray eyes.

I smoothed the dress out as best as I could as I walked into the incredibly white and quiet room. There was the weird abstract art I had pictured in my head. The scrawls looked like a child had done them, yet they were selling for millions.

I walked up to a strange painting of a girl in a corner, her back against a copied image of herself. The image made me feel scared and uneasy. It was black and grey with streaks of red strewn around it. The whole thing made me feel really uncomfortable. Cringing, I turned to leave and ran right into a suited gentleman, spilling what remained of my drink on him.

"Sorry," I apologized awkwardly, wiping off his suit jacket. He stared at me, and when I realized I was wiping at absolutely nothing but my own shame, I dropped my hand.

He peeked at his suit jacket and smirked at me.

"Enjoying the view?" he drawled, his voice a husky rasp that made me shiver. He looked familiar, but I doubted I knew someone this good-looking.

"It's interesting," I said, looking over at the creepy canvas.

He chuckled, the sound rumbling and musical.

Where the fuck did I know this guy from?

"My favorite is definitely 'The Streams of Red' portrait. I rather enjoy the mixing of white and red," he continued a curious glint in his eyes. "Sometimes black and red make the best combination."

I raised my eyebrow, not understanding his joke about himself.

Whatever.

"Well...have a good night," I said and started to turn away. He caught my arm, staring into my eyes with lustful promise. "You too. I'll catch you later."

Shivers ran down my spine as the gorgeous man walked out, his black curly hair giving a tip to a Middle Eastern heritage.

"Hey! You're Carrie's sister, right?" I blinked, pulling my gaze from the stranger and instead meeting the stare of Pedro Maltiez.

He was handsome as far as ruthless killers went. He had nice features, and he weirdly seemed nice, with warmness in his gaze. It could be a ruse.

"Hi, yes. I'm Ella Forest. Nice to meet you...Pedro?"

I had changed my last name to Forest just in case he had decided to do any digging. The last thing I needed was him snooping around and finding out I was actually a doctor of psychology for the Rochester Police Department.

"I've heard a lot about you. We have a lot of mutual interests," he said, grabbing my arm and leading me to the back wall of artistry.

"Oh yeah? Like what?" I said, genuinely curious. Cassie had told me the basics of what she'd said to these guys, but I wouldn't have guessed that what she'd said to him was remotely similar.

"We both have dramatic siblings, for one." He laughed, and I joined him.

"Yeah, you could say that for sure. Carrie is a mess." I'd agreed to use Cassie's alias.

I caught sight of a pamphlet. It held the smiling face of an arrogant devil on the front.

"Son of a bitch!" That was the devil...standing in front of me like it was no big deal. Ugh!

Scrambling to the window, I gawked around until I spotted him. He was swaggering back into his damn club, and I was sure he was floating on a cloud of his own ego from knowing I had to be the cop demanding to see his rude ass.

Pedro eyed me, but whatever. Curiosity and confusion mangled into one thought as I swore louder at the window and started tapping on it. "You bastard!"

After a few deep breaths, I turned back to Pedro. "Sorry, I need to go."

He nodded, an odd smirk on his face. I'd have to think about his reaction later, and I took off, sprinting after Lucius, mother fucking, Vasiliev.

Arriving at the doors, I screamed at Vasiliev, who saw me and winked while signaling for his meat-head bodyguards to shut the door in my face again. I shrieked. Anger flooded through me. This fucker wasn't going to get away so easily.

I crept around the alley, wrinkling my nose at the images of those guys being murdered here prior. Crouching down, I planted my butt on the cemented ground and prepared to wait all night until the asshole left the place.

A few hours later, my resolve was fading, and I was about to leave with my tail between my damn legs when a masculine cry sounded from the other side of the door to *Black Mirrors*. The sound was muffled, but I was indeed hearing the cry of pain. Another shriek sounded. It wasn't just one person but multiple. Was I hearing female screams mixed in there, too? Damnit, I was…

Alarmed, I peered through the glass of the door. Blurred images of a dark-skinned man, bleeding and tied up near the bar, came into view. He was being worked over by a dark shadow, rendering more of those screams.

What the fuck?

Pulling the pin from the dress, I twisted it and used it to pick the lock on the door. With a silent click, it gave way and popped open. The cries of the man continued to echo off the walls as I crouched in the corners, moving closer to his location.

"This hurts me, too, little dwarf." I heard a faint voice say. "For once, I don't want to do this, but she's taunting me, my friend, and I can't have that."

The dark bronze-skinned man coated in crimson-red blood said, "You ain't gotta do this, man. I didn't do anything to you. Please."

The shadowy figure sighed, straightening his back before walking out of the bar area. He kept going until he went through a random door in the corner of the room near the dance floor. My heart pounded as I grabbed my boot knife and walked toward the battered male.

"What?" he whimpered when he finally saw me leave the safety of the shadows.

He wept even harder. I was his rescue. His reaction made me think that he felt sincere relief in his soul. "I'm sorry! I'm so sorry," he said, his voice breaking.

I smiled weakly. "You have nothing to apologize for. Shhh…."

He tried to quiet his sobs, helping untie his feet as I sliced the rope off his other hand.

"Who did this to you?" I whispered, releasing the last of the binds and helping him to his feet.

He gave me a scared look before his gaze shifted toward the room where the shadow had disappeared. I gave him a gentle squeeze and pointed to the back door I had opened, putting my finger to my lips as he gave me an apologetic grin one last time and shuffled for the door.

I stepped back into the shadows, my back plastered against the wall, a damn mirror reflecting my image back at me and bouncing off another mirror across the way.

I'm a sitting duck here.

My survival instinct grappled with my need for justice as I finally turned my back, approaching the door I had entered.

Nausea bubbled in my throat, and I felt the awful sensation of dizziness creep over my body. It finally froze me into place right outside the door's entrance.

What is happening to me?

I tried to shake it off and keep running, but my legs felt like cement was starting to leak into them, and I knew then that I wasn't going to make it.

Oh god, had I been drugged?

My vision began to fade, black spots dancing in front of my eyes. I felt my body slam forward, smashing my ribcage into the dumpster.

Drugs in my drink over there. It…was…only explanation.

I sank down because my legs were completely useless. Landing on my arm, I flinched. There was a puncture wound on my bicep.

What the hell?

Forcing my body to move, I pulled myself underneath the cover of the slimy dumpster, and I could only helplessly watch as my world surrendered to the darkness.

Chapter 12

Ember

*T*ugging.
 Pulling.

I opened my eyes, and the darkness completely surrounded me. My head pounded. After getting into my tent for the night, I didn't remember a thing, but my head felt like an anvil had been dropped onto it. Did someone from the cove clock me? Voices. They were fuzzy. My vision was completely useless at the moment as the pain of rough gravel scraped along my back.

"Oh no. No, Little Princess. You're not waking up just yet."

The voice faded, like it was talking under water, deep and unfamiliar, and suddenly the blasting pain in my head increased before I succumbed to it.

I struggled with the restraints. My wrists and ankles were aching at the binds.

Who dared to kidnap me?

My vision was fuzzy even more than before I'd first awoken to these assholes. Whoever it was had me in the dark again, and I couldn't tell where I was at all. The only thing I noticed was a slight smell of salt in the air.

Hot breath wafted in my face as a man laughed. "Looky what we caught, boss."

I glared toward the sound of a squeaking door, the light penetrating from that direction. A hulking frame was highlighted in the doorway, its fuzzy appearance blocking most of the light.

My eyes watered, and my head throbbed. I was naked. The cool air was chilling my skin, and I had been bound in a more degrading pose than a stuck pig. My hands were tied to my ankles, and my back was forced to bow at a painful angle. I pushed at the cloth in my mouth, trying to prevent my gag reflex from taking over from the salty-tinged garment.

"Indeed, looks like we found you first, then," another male said —this one younger and handsome in some warped way.

"Does the boss know about this?" Yet another guy asked from behind me. I hadn't even noticed him. "He wanted to play with this one."

The guy at the door scoffed.

"I don't give a fuck what the boss wants. I'm tired of this little runt picking us off. She had already found us. Do you want to wait to be snuffed out?"

I smiled through the cloth, letting them know it was one hundred percent what I intended to do as soon as I could free myself.

Someone lit a match, and an ancient lantern created a glow around me. I was in some kind of cavern. Maybe even a closed-off section of my own damned home. The wall closest to me had that stucco cave texture in appearance, and I was sure if I would run my hand along it, I would feel that scraping rough gravel.

Take a woman from her own bed? How manly of you.

"I don't know about this, Pedro," the mousy one said, shifting from one foot to another.

"Look, she was looking for me, trying to kill Markus. I don't care if she's a damn woman. I will have fun with her, and then it's lights out for this chick."

I was biting my tongue so hard I tasted blood.

Shit.

I needed to figure out a way to get out of this. I was completely stripped of my weapons, including my damn clothes. Except for my broken nails, I didn't have anything to use. Panic was an annoying, sour taste in my mouth, so I forced my body to settle with it.

"Geer, you go guard the entrance to this shithole," the one named Pedro barked.

He walked up to me, my body pathetically dangling from the bar I was hung on.

"Too bad you're on the wrong side of this," he said, shaking his head and kicking my leg. The bar wobbled, swinging me back and forth.

The sound of the old contraption was a scraping metal on corroded metal. This was going to suck…but it was the only idea I had to get myself out of here. I successfully spit out the cloth, my blood tinging the tip red.

"If you give me a sob story about how we could take on the world by drugging people into mindless zombies, I'm going to puke," I said, tightening my stomach for what I knew was coming.

The guys in the back chuckled, their laughter dying with the look that Pedro shot them.

He met my gaze and glared. "Okay, we'll do this the fun way then."

His big foot smashed hard into my ribs, and the instant feeling of breathing broken glass blazed through my body as the mechanism shook and groaned. I stifled myself from coughing, spitting blood in his direction.

He chuckled. "You are a feisty one. I would have liked to fuck that rebellion out of you."

"Too bad I don't go for shrimp dicks. The last guy who tried ate his." I said, forcing a laugh. "Literally." I chomped my teeth for reference.

His face flushed, and I knew I had hit home. My effort of scraping my raw wrists against the rusted pole was progressing. The binds were loosening.

There was no preparing myself for this hit, however. The kick was so hard it spun my body over the pole five times before slamming me hard onto my stomach and freeing the binding on my arm. I wrapped my forearm and freed my leg around the metal, refusing to be flipped back around.

I could hear the internal clicking and crackling increase from the metal contraption, so at least my pain was not going to be in vain.

"You certainly have a hot little mouth on you, oh mighty Snow White," he cooed, running his ugly hand along my jaw.

I shivered.

"I wonder if you are hot and untamable in other areas."

I couldn't see his eyes, but I felt them graze over my flesh, my only warning before his cold finger invaded my body. I forced the unwanted invasion out of my mind because it was unimportant at this point. Even with my vision dotted with white from being walloped and my body screaming at me, I knew I had to finish this, and I had to do it now before he explored me further.

I steeled myself as best I could, knowing this final blow would force me unconscious. If that happened, I would be killed, and before that...I didn't want to think about what these barbarians intended to do with me. Alive or dead.

Right before I managed to quip my last remark, a sound of pain exploded from outside the cave. Pedro spun around, and the other men were scrambling and running off to see the cause of the commotion. The screams of agony were like a symphony—a crescendo playing in my ears.

I tried to keep focus. My vision was still blurry as a familiar face came into view.

He was covered in blood.

His clothes were shredded, cuts and scrapes marring his beautiful body. Pedro whirled around, cowering before the manifestation of pure menace and rage.

"Your first mistake was touching what is mine," he bellowed.

His booming roar shook the restraints and the metal as the hinges collapsed, making me crash down onto the ground and smash my ankles and wrists with my own weight. The pain sobered me enough to see clearly as Lucius, the pale Russian ghost, bit off the finger that the fuck had used to violate me and used his bare hands to rip his head off.

"Your second mistake was thinking you would get away with it."

He cracked the bones of the digit in his mouth before spitting it out onto the ground. The crunching pop was a jolting sound as the blood poured onto my body from the man's severed head, a crimson waterfall that was sure to drown me.

I weakly crawled up the pole and pulled my hands free of the metal. Lucius looked down on me. The blood surrounding me mirrored his eyes. He was close enough that I could see my reflection in those pools of green.

"You are mine. You can't escape me." He growled at me while throwing the head of the man at the wall behind me.

I flinched as more blood splattered my body. I wanted to glare at him but was too busy trying to free myself. I wasn't up for fighting. My ribs burned, and I needed time to heal. He tilted his head, his gaze flashing as he stared at my naked body. Anger and lust were a constant swirl on his blood-stained features.

Freeing my legs finally, I eyed the exit. It was behind him. How was I going to get past him?

He followed my gaze and smiled, his black hair dripping from the blood of his enemies.

"Planning to run Little Shadow? What kind of thanks is that?" He tsked, pulling off his shirt and wiping the blood from his face. He threw the mangled T-shirt to the side. "Just remember, I love it when you run from me. It'll make your submission much more potent when I catch you."

I laughed as best I could while trying to ignore the stabbing pain in my ribs. "I was doing pretty well myself. You didn't have to maul the other hunters. I would have done that, you egotistical asshat."

He snorted. His musical laughter lilted with the fury coiled in his big muscular body.

"Oh, Little Shadow, make no mistake." Crouching down and running a gentle hand down my cheek. "You've always been mine to kill. There are no other hunters. Just you and me."

His caressing hands suddenly gripped my neck, pushing me down hard yet still somehow cradling my head from harm.

He mounted my body, his powerful build caging me underneath him. Besides his hand at my throat, he wasn't touching me. I couldn't decide at that moment if I was happy about that or not. His lips were so close to mine. I suddenly froze. I was not able to think clearly, but then, out of the corner of my eye, I saw a shining light from a crack in the wall.

Instantly, I knew where I was and how to be free. Truly free. Looking into the eyes of my monster, I filled the space, my lips going flush against his. The taste of blood, sweat, and pure heat radiated in my mouth.

It made me dizzy, my body not prepared to flood with warmth

and go lax against his naked chest. I could tell Lucius felt the same way as his body relaxed, his hand falling away from my neck to steady himself on the ground.

His eyes closed, and he deepened the kiss. His tongue battled mine, twisting, sucking, and biting. His hand slid between my thighs, my wetness, and the enemy's blood dripped from me. Sliding between the folds of my pussy, slipping the blood over my clit.

Shaking my resolve, he groaned in my ear. "I always thought you looked beautiful in red. But now, bathed in your enemies' blood, your cunt is so wet and ready for me. You. Look. Radiant. I need to feel you. I need to see that smile of pure ecstasy on your face again. I need it almost as much as I need your life."

I twisted my body away from him, the pain in my side sobering me, pulling him back down to me, savoring the taste of him one last second. I reached for the metal pipe and smashed it into the wall above me.

Hearing Lucius's confused outrage, I took a deep breath and dove under the crumbling wall. Finally, away from his heat, his damning taste and touch, and straight into the icy waters below, cleared my focus fast.

Chapter 13

Lucius

The wall was crumbling around me like dominoes. I roared, searching for my Little Shadow. I refused to believe that she escaped me again. My head was still spinning from her lips, and the pure taste of her…she was intoxicating.

Toxic.

Her very own poison.

I picked up the rocks, flinging them to the side, blindly searching for her in the dust.

Gaaahh…Where did she go?

Coughing from the continued cloud of debris, I finally retreated, running out of the cave and up to the city floor to breathe in fresh air. Looking like something out of a Halloween movie covered in blood and dust, I hightailed it back to the club. Markus was there. His arrogance was as clear as day. He certainly didn't look the part for someone known as The Butcher.

"Don't you know it's not nice annoying someone in their own home?" I griped, walking past him to the bar and scrubbing my hands to rid them of the dried blood.

Markus never liked being ignored. His ballooning ego would never allow it.

He pretended like I hadn't spoken.

"Oh, always the diligent soldier, aren't you, Lucy Bell?" I glared. The nickname pissed me off. "Why do you look like 'Carrie,' from that horror movie anyway?" Markus pointed at me, plopping down onto a barstool and leaning over to watch me sink my arms halfway into the sanitizing basin behind the bar.

I wondered if any of the blood I was washing away was from my Little Shadow.

She didn't look injured when I arrived, but I couldn't be sure. It was so damn dark in that hole. Perfect for her size, but I had been swinging madly at nothing, and I was only lucky to catch the shit-stain men who'd captured her.

Why the fuck they thought they had any right to manhandle my Little Shadow...

Mine. Not theirs.

The pink marks from their thick fingers on her porcelain white skin had me seeing red. And Pedro—he'd overstepped big fucking time. Not only had he stripped my Little Shadow naked, showing her lushly perfect curves, but he'd marred those curves with his disgusting boot.

He deserved more than what he'd gotten. The need to go back to that crumbled tunnel and smash his severed head until it became red paint for my walls was amplified.

"Are you really going to keep ignoring me?"

I snapped my head up. My murderous instinct made my body vibrate, and my glare stopped on the man who was too stupid to see just how much I needed to kill.

"What do you want, Markus," I wiped my hands and arms with a white cloth, soaking it to a blackened maroon. "Or should I say, 'The Butcher?' "

He didn't appreciate my musings, and his eyes narrowed with suspicion. I couldn't give a shit.

"I said, your father is not happy about all the shit you have stirred up. There's a serial killer who has been culling us like fowl for years, and you were moved here to catch them. The fact that you haven't just shows how incompetent you are. Your father decided I was best suited to take over the task. That includes your precious club. Not that it's staying a club. I really think bringing the skin trade over here will work. A brothel of sorts," he continued to drone on.

My ears were not picking up much after he claimed Daddy Dearest wanted to dethrone me.

Are you kidding me?

I was the fucking king of this fucking castle, and so what if I didn't kill the Little Shadow. Yet. I was going to. As any good killer knew, learning their victim's weaknesses was the key to their undoing.

After planting the cameras in her underground hovel, I could see every single weakness of hers as they wandered around, setting up their new tents and puking from overeating the extra food she'd given them. It was apparent they weren't used to eating very much.

I planned to break down the Little Shadow by slicing up every one of her dwarves.

"I wish you good luck if you think you're going to take what I've built from nothing," I said to Markus, feeling nothing, empty, void.

"I thought you'd say that. And while I know it would be great to cleave your pretty boy body to bits finally, I have an offer instead." Narrowing my eyes and leaning lazily on the bar, I nodded. "Alyosha is expecting me to run things here now so you and I can 'share' for the time being."

I snorted. In Russia, where I grew up until I was five, I didn't share. I stabbed some kid with a pencil for trying to take one of my toys. Now, being the type of man that I was, I liked to share even less.

"Think about it, Lucius," he said, eyeing me. "Boss said you've got a pending investigation for a murder that happened outside. They need a warrant, but they'll get one eventually. They will go through all the receipts and figure out that this is a front, and they are going to find all the dirty money."

I contemplated that. It had been a few weeks since the detectives were trying to bust down my door. My guards, Kaipo and Reggie, said they practically had to assault one of them to get them to fucking relent. Not pigs, pigs were stupid, but detectives were like vultures, the lot of them. They were just waiting for a chance to strike.

"If I let you stay in a spare room, you tell my father to use a Yakutian as a dildo."

I had to smile slightly at the memory of my Little Shadow orgasming so beautifully from her own little dagger.

Markus pulled at his collar, the image making him sweat a bit. Despite being called The Butcher, the guy was more like The Bitcher. His lackeys would do all the fun parts, and he took credit, never actually getting his uncalloused hands dirty.

"Right," he said primly.

The preppy fuck flopped down on my favorite couch exactly where she'd left the best part of her pleasure. I growled, the involuntary sound leaving my throat and startling Markus as much as it did me.

Markus jumped up from the couch, staring at me. I, however, was focused on the spot.

Her spot.

Our spot.

Not his.

"Get your disgusting ass away from my couch," I said.

My control was slipping, and my tone proved it. I did not have a grasp on my normal. Was this a new normal? I glanced back at

Markus, perplexed. He turned, looking at the couch, confusion causing his bushy black eyebrows to bunch together.

"This piece of shit is stained with whatever you killed on it," he said, disgusted, as he moved to a bar stool instead.

I clenched my teeth so hard I could almost feel them cracking as I moved so fast I was at his side within seconds.

"What did you say?" He would not speak about her that way.

He blinked up at me, his expression finally understanding the amount of danger he was in.

To his credit, he did try to move his hand, but I was faster. My Little Shadow's dagger plunged into his flesh and bone, anchoring him to the bar top.

He screamed.

I yawned and grumbled. "Your hand is fucking up my bar, Markus. I just cleaned the damn thing, and look...now, you're getting it all bloody again."

Markus's muddy eyes stared at me, watching me grab a bottle of bleach and dump it on the bartop and his hand. His wound turned as ghostly white as his face. His screams nearly cracked the mirror closest to the bar area.

Digging my finger in my ear to readjust my eardrums back to normal, I walked around the bar to stand next to him. He finally quieted and passed out on the marbled stone.

Looking over his deathly still form, I shuddered as pure menace filled my being. I pulled the dagger from his hand. His form jolted like a live wire, the pain acting as a shot of adrenaline. To my delight, it didn't bleed.

"Listen here, partner," I said, my voice lilting and falling like a lullaby. "That couch. That stain. This club. Are all mine."

Markus just nodded and then looked at the bleach bubbling up on his open wound and the skin on his hand. His phone rang, and he looked at me. I nodded.

Answering, he said, "Yeah, bring her in."

Confused, I watched the door as it opened, and two guys from Markus's little posse walked in. A sleeping form was being dragged into the center of them. Looking at Markus again, my eyes said it all. Who the fuck was this woman? Markus cradled his injury, wincing as he tried to smile.

"I brought you a gift, Lucius."

I didn't give a shit about women, much less a gift-wrapped one. Sleeping females didn't do a fucking thing for my dick. Honestly, the only person who had even gotten the fucking thing to stir was my Little Shadow.

I looked at the female. A white gag was in her mouth. She had some cuts on her face and bruises on her wrists, but otherwise, she was unmarked. A small cascade of brown curls framed her face. Her lips were smeared with a red rouge. She was beautiful, but there were a million beautiful women.

"Uh, thanks?" I flicked the heels of the platform black heels she had on with boredom.

"You don't understand," Markus said, his voice steadier now. His excitement showed at knowing something that I didn't.

"This is an escort and not just any escort. She's the one who flipped on me. I have clientele in law enforcement, and I found out this bitch has a sister in the department. One they set up with one of my boys."

The pieces started to fall into place. Pedro was at the Art Galla. I noticed him after I finished my fun. I didn't say anything to him, not really giving a fuck what he did with his spare time.

When I found him kidnapping my Little Shadow, that was another thing entirely. I decided not to mention that 'his boy' was rat chow and let him continue.

"She knows about the rings. Hell, she may even know about you and Moya Kotova. I caught her sniffing around, and she was asking me shit when I was with her. I gave her a bogus address, and now we're just waiting to catch the bitch's cop sister too."

I looked at the light brown-haired girl again. I didn't kill women often. I left a prostitute to fuck with my Little Shadow, but she was a double for my operation, and I figured I'd get a two-birds kind of deal out of it. Listening to the stream of curses and learning that this princess had become the maid had been fun, but I was done now.

"So?" Markus said, waiting for a pat on the ass.

"So." I simply shrugged. "Don't get blood on my floor."

Ignoring him, I pulled up my CCTV footage on my phone, snatched the bottle of Macallan from the cracked table, and walked back to my room.

Chapter 14

Ella

I called for the fifteenth time, getting nothing but the cheery tone of my sister's voicemail.

"Cassie, it's me. Again. Look, please don't pull a Houdini, okay? I'm sorry I bailed on the druggie. I got distracted...but anyway, I'm super worried about you. So much shit is happening, and I just need to know you're okay. All right. Well, I'm keeping my phone on me, so please text me. I love you, Cassandra Fox. So much. I'd be lost without you."

I walked around. Mitzi and Shadow tried curling up at my feet, but I couldn't stop pacing. My old-fashioned clock was as loud as ever in my ears. Worse yet, I was trying to figure out how in the hell to have this conversation with Quinn without giving away too much of my dumb-assery.

I couldn't tell him I bailed on my date with a known cartel drug mule or that my lovely sister, who was now fucking missing, set it up.

I couldn't tell him I saved a civilian from the club I had no right to be in or that I had been stalking the owner of said club.

No, I was in what Cassie called a 'fuckity-fuck-pie.' I chewed on my lip. Feeling the blood coat my tongue.

Picking up my phone to dial Quinn's number, I stopped. The

door buzzer for my apartment was going off. Begrudgingly, I looked out the window, seeing his pretty scruff of blond hair. Taking a deep breath and forcing my body to get its shit together, I buzzed him up.

Opening the door to off-duty Micah Quinn was a pleasant surprise. The ripped blue jeans and silky dark blue shirt that matched his eyes really threw me off even more.

"Hey, Ella. You look nice today."

"Uh, thanks. You too, Quinn." I blushed, staring at my converse. The truth was that I just put on a shit ton of makeup to hide my bruises. I did a number on my body from falling into the freaking dumpster. My face and stomach were all scratched up from my lovely faceplant. Thank god for the high-end foundation my sister stashed in my bathroom.

He smiled, his blinding pearly whites popping out, and his fingers worried through his neatly shaven beard.

"Call me Micah. We're not at the station." He reached out and tucked his fingertip under my chin. "Everything okay?" he said.

The silence stretched awkwardly as that damn clock ticked in the background. As soon as he left, I planned to rip the thing off my wall and smash it to pieces. I caught my reflection in the mirror hanging on the bathroom door. A vision of my sister's smiling face taunted me. Her crooked smile hitched up the corner of her mouth.

"Uh, no." I finally said, sighing in defeat. "My sister may be missing."

Quinn, always the kind soldier, snapped to attention. He pulled out his pen and tiny notebook he kept in his pocket out of habit from being in law enforcement.

"When did you last see her? And I need a description of her." He held his pen to his pad, ready to write.

I sighed and walked over to my bathroom, grabbing the picture of my beautiful sister and handing it numbly to the man I knew would find her. With everything in me, I just hoped we would locate her soon.

"She's a hooker," I blurted out, word vomit style. Staring at me with a mix of compassion and confusion, Quinn cleared his throat.

"Uh, okay. Well, do you know what circles she works in?"

I racked my brain, struggling to remember vital information that would help the investigation.

"Yeah, I think so. She's higher ranked than the streets. She does escort detail with high profile clients...people you don't want to know about." I added, watching Detective Quinn blow out an unsure breath.

"I have to ask," he said at last. "Is there anyone I know?"

I scrunched my nose in disgust. Unable to filter my thoughts. Begrudgingly, I muttered, "Chief Doger."

Now Quinn made a face. His perfectly featured face looked repulsed and had me laughing. I was unable to hide my snort.

"Yeah, okay, better left unsaid," he agreed, his face was now tinted green.

I laughed harder, my unease and worry fading just the slightest bit with Quinn by my side. His kind eyes and strong jaw just made a person feel more at ease. He was such a sweet man who had been through so much. He was the definition of the notion of 'light still shining through darkness.' Micah Quinn was a fucking beacon of sunshine and...my friend.

Guilt settled in my gut like a train, so I chewed on my ruined lip even more.

"What'd you do, Ella Fox?" he said at last, studying me and giving me a tone that could rival any fantastic big brother.

I took the collar of my halter top, pulling it up over my nose. It was a nervous habit I'd done since I was a child. The action made me feel safe.

"C'mon. It's okay. Come out of your shell, Ella. No need to turtle." He snickered at my glare.

I couldn't think of a dumb thing to change his last name to, so I sighed and relented my escape.

"Okay, fine," I whined, sounding every bit like the child still hidden inside me. "I may have been stalking the owner of *Black Mirrors*…"

His face looked stern, but he allowed me to continue.

Taking a deep breath, I said, "And I may have heard something from inside the club, picked the lock with a hairpin my sister clipped in my boobs for a weird date she set up to try to help, which didn't, and I left him anyway. Also, my date is actually part of the drug ring we're chasing, and when I snuck into the club, there may have been a young man who needed my help—just a teenager, maybe nineteen or twenty."

I sighed, not wanting to continue, but did so when he cocked his head to the side and urged me to keep talking with a simple lift of his chin.

"And, I may have saved him and run off, only to randomly pass out in a dumpster and wake up in a ton of pain because of my own stupidity. And I didn't tell you because I know I fucked up and may be a horrible person."

After I finished my word vomit session, I just waited and waited as Quinn took what was only probably a minute to process my words, but it felt like an hour. He kept eyeing me as he thought, his face making all kinds of expressions, none of them great.

I just stared at him sheepishly.

"Then we need to go find your sister. Now."

My mouth gaped. He was going to help me? Off books? He could lose his badge for this. Hell, we could be thrown behind bars with the prisoners we put there.

"Yes, Ella," he said, standing and brushing off imaginary lint from his Armani shirt.

"I'll send a message to Blue about the John you saved. Maybe there will be a missing person report for him, and maybe his attackers will try to get him back. I'll have an APB set for his description and have some guys follow him if they do find him."

"I can't tell them he was found at *Black Mirrors* because you weren't authorized to be there..." he said, scratching his head, obviously still thinking. "In the meantime, you need to get a brown wig and front as your sister. Maybe someone will know something about where she may have been before she disappeared."

I looked down at my Converse and my black leggings. "Actually..."

Quinn looked at me now. Exasperation was all over his beautiful features.

"I have an address for a local warehouse The Butcher is supposed to own..."

He gave the slightest twitch to his jaw but said nothing else. He just tucked the picture of me and my sister in his dark jeans and held open the door.

The street was actually fucking cold. It was supposed to be summer, and I couldn't feel my ass cheeks in this ridiculous micro mini skirt. The brown-haired wig on my head itched to all high hell, and the girls wanted absolutely nothing to do with me.

Trying another alley, I walked to the street where the girls congregated. Some were hanging their heads in the car windows of shady drivers. Others were off to the side smoking a cigarette. I chose the latter.

"Hey!" I said, trying to impersonate my best Cassie voice.

"How are you guys…girls hanging tonight?"

The prostitutes looked me over, assessing me from my clunky ass heels to the top of my short head. They didn't have to look long.

"Girl, are you new?"

Internally cursing at myself, I forced a laugh. "Nah, silly. I'm Cas—Carrie."

They continued to inspect me quietly.

"Thought you were too big for the streets, baby girl," a woman said, stepping out from the crowd.

I laughed dramatically, wincing at my own volume.

"No, I am just with you girls tonight. I know…I had some big clients last week, but I forgot their names. I know. Silly me! Did any of you happen to catch the Johns's names?"

The lady eyed me suspiciously—her over-done makeup and marred skin from hard work gleamed in the overhead lamps on the street.

"If I didn't know any better," she said, her thickly mascaraed eyes pinning me down. "I'd say you sound like a cop sniffing for details."

The other women gasped, scattering like pins to a bowling ball with the word cop. The cars lined-up on the street sped off, leaving rubber marks and exhaust fumes. I glanced over at the blue sedan. Quinn shook his head at the wheel at me.

Well fuck.

Angry at myself, I ripped off the damned wig.

"I'm not here to bust anyone, okay?" I said in my tone, my eyes pleading with the woman who stayed behind.

"I'm just here to find my sister. She hasn't answered her phone and had a shady client last week. I'm worried."

The woman chuckled dryly, flicking on a cheap, red lighter and touching it to the tip of her cigarette. "All Johns are shady, hunny. You need to do better than that."

I ground my molars. I was annoyed at this lady and half wanted to slap some cuffs on her. Shiny metal ones.

"He went by the name The Butcher," I said through clenched teeth.

She took a hit and blew out the smoke in my face. "Oh, that's Markus Moshkov. He owns a butcher shop out on Lakeshore Ave," she said, waving her hand and turning around. "Now, since you've scared off my money for the night, you can give me what I would have made."

I stared at her. Her wrinkly aging skin, a pound of makeup, and weight under her sparkly bra forced me to keep my mouth shut. This lady couldn't make more than between twenty and fifty dollars a night.

Quinn got out of the car, his hair slicked back and his calloused hands flipping through a wad of bills from his fancy black wallet. Shoving well over five hundred dollars at the old hag, he grabbed my arm and hauled me back to the car.

I started protesting. Saying she didn't deserve that at all, but he put his finger to my lips, halting any other argument.

"Quiet, Ella. It's for her silence," he said.

"Now," he continued, staring up at the car. "Let's go find us, The Butcher."

Chapter 15

Ember

I smiled at the man. His name was John or something like that. He was a nice enough lay, I guess, but the credit card I neatly stuck in my boot was better. It got me all the way to the beach.

I didn't often resort to stealing from attractive civilians, but lately, I had to keep a low profile. Killing five dealers in one night set a scattering effect. Meaning that if I wasn't careful, I knew that anyone left would leave.

Sighing, I kicked at a shell on the beach with my foot. I was a good-ways out of the city. Lake Erie had a nice little beach that didn't have a ton of people on it, and there were enough small islands near the bank that I found a lot of ground untouched by anyone else.

It was how I had found that beach cop. Admittedly, I had a thing for men in uniform, and the thrill of knowing my own little secret had me buzzing. Unfortunately, I couldn't get that fuckhead out of my mind. Lucius Vasiliev. That bastard had given me lady blue balls. Now, anyone else who tried to touch me could do nothing. I couldn't get off at all with Mister Popo. All I managed to do was chafe my skin with scratchy sand and collect a ton of questionable water where it didn't belong.

My anger was growing, so I got up and dusted off my white bikini. Trying to shake the sand off my ass, I decided taking a dip in the water would be the more effective. Going outside the normal beach area, past a small sandy island, I stopped at a palm tree someone clearly had planted a long time ago. Surprised it actually grew, I patted the trunk.

"We both don't belong here, do we?" I mused aloud.

Feeling annoyed at how itchy I felt, I peeked around the little shrubbery and a few trees. Only seeing people way off in the distance, I shimmied out of the crunchy bathers and smacked them against the palm tree, using all my irritation at what that asshole took from me. Why couldn't I just orgasm once with a perfectly acceptable dude?

Glaring a hole in the tiny white crotchet suit, I gave up, dropping it and wading myself into the chilled waters.

Doing a makeshift wash and feeling more like I was using those soaps from nail salons instead, I finally resorted to just floating on the top of the water. Enjoying the sunshine on my skin, I closed my eyes and breathed a peaceful sigh.

Sure enough, my peace dissipated when I heard shuffling from behind the foliage.

Squinting, trying to see past the lush green of the big bushes and small trees, I yelled, "Hey, get out of my shit, you rodent!"

Stupid trash pandas were notorious around here because the sandbar was right on the water. Also, the bar got a ton of traction, including some of the nosiest woodland critters.

Despite this dumb town calling me Snow White, I couldn't sing a note or communicate with animals. Hell, I tried to sing as a kid since Dad always called me his princess, but my valiant efforts always ended with me having to get a tetanus immunoglobin injection.

No thanks.

The bushes continued to move, the sound of that wood-cracking scuffle amping my annoyance even more. So, I swam back to shore, not needing some skunk to spray my stuff or a squirrel to run off with it.

When I arrived on the little island, I felt a strange sense creep up my neck. There was a sour taste caught in the current, and I knew by now what that was. Precisely as predicted, a body lay crumpled up at an awkward angle, beaten, bloody, and missing a few things.

Gagging, I realized this lump of meat used to be a male…and now, among his male parts, he was also missing his hands, the whole section of his jaw and tongue, and a whole random pattern skinned off his thighs, stomach, chest, and forearms.

Squinting to focus, I suddenly recognized that this was the cop I had been with last night. His entire body was nearly unrecognizable. The skinned-off areas were the places that had touched me. Searching for what may have done this, I was in awe at the artistry of precision in how the body was mastered.

It was sad. This guy was just a cop who, as far as I knew, didn't do anything to deserve this slice-and-dice death. Plus, I could tell by the way the blood had pooled and coated him that he hadn't been dead before the flaying was done.

I didn't see anyone around, but what caught my eye was something sticking up from the sand. Walking over to it, I leaned down and saw the cop's two dismembered hands. Gasping in outrage, I cursed. Carved in the palms of the flesh and neatly printed were the words "Miss" and "Me."

Steam was practically rolling off of me in waves. That fucking asshole thought he could torture some sad sack and leave me a message? Ha! No.

I wasn't playing his game or giving him the satisfaction of ruining my 'sexcation.'

I stalked back to the beach, leaving the body right where he'd left it. Finding four random good-looking guys lazily lounging on the beach, I pulled one to me.

I planted a sloppy, ungracious kiss on his lips. Grabbing the next one's hand, I sucked on his finger. Finally, I ran my fingertips down his chest to his dick. The last one, I didn't touch. He just watched the encounter with lust-fueled eyes.

Leaving them dazed but not feeling so much as a flutter for myself, I smirked, my smile defiant more than anything, and walked off to the sandbar.

After getting dressed, the crowds here by the boardwalk were ridiculous, but at least the food was delicious. I ordered a crab special and started dozing off at the lull of idiots droning on about their mundane lives.

"Ahh! Oh my god!"

A woman's screams had me jolting up, trying to get a view of whatever was in the water. The whole restaurant was gawking, yelling, and pointing. Was there a shark or something?

My short ass couldn't see anything, so I stepped up onto my table and peered over the heads of the others. As I figured, I couldn't see much of anything, so I sighed and hopped down. I was ready to leave and give up on the hours of waiting, but then the overhead speakers crackled.

"Where is finger? Where is finger? Oh, here I am." Then, it

switched, and I heard, "Oh my, what beautiful eyes you have…all the better to ogle you with, my dear…I see you."

And then there was nothing. The speakers went dead.

Everyone was screaming and running around like rats.

Before I even went down to the shoreline, I knew what would be floating in the water. Refusing to walk down to confirm, I stubbornly sat back down in my seat. A waiter walked over and set down my tray.

"Finally," I grumbled, lifting up the lid. However, it was not my crab special.

It was a dried-up tongue. My guess from the guy on the island. Burned into the fleshy mounds of it, "Careful Snow, those delicious lips of yours are dangerous. Everything you touch will feel my poison."

Snarling, I threw it off the table and used the chaos as cover to leave the bar. Taking two steps at a time, I practically used my rage to float me back over to the island. It was dusk now, and the sun was finally dipping behind the water line.

I stubbed my toe on stupid rocks as I tried to navigate my way back by memory. It wasn't hard once the stink of a cooking body caught my nose. Sure enough, the devil himself was leaning on a tree. His triumphant smile beaming was annoying, and he was covered in blood.

His shirt dripped blood onto the cool sand.

He was not, however, wearing pants.

My eyes involuntarily bugged at the size of him. I had caught glimpses of his cock before in the club with his whole knife-play situation. But it had been contained behind pants. It was a bit intimidating at the time, but now, seeing it free and hardening, he caught my gaze. It was hard not to blush.

I felt myself getting wet, the heat pooling at my center, my white bikini doing nothing to hide my approval of him.

"Like my gifts, Little Shadow?" His voice was husky and thick with need.

"No," I growled, reaching back to steady myself.

He was stalking me like the predator that he was. I cleared my throat, backing up from him and twisting at an angle to avoid the dead body on the ground. He was cornering me into the palm tree and the water.

I could turn around and run, but I was liable to fall into a hole of deep water. It was a minefield out here from the erosion of the sand and the water below it. Never knew when you'd sink into an eighteen-foot sinkhole.

Why was he still wearing a shirt?

No. I mean, why didn't he have pants on?

He made a face of mock sadness and chuckled. "Didn't figure you for fucking a pig," he said, a more serious tone in his voice.

I scoffed.

"Like you know anything about me." I challenged.

Lucius was too close now. His finger ran a slow trail across my jawline, his touch teasing the center of my chest. My nipples hardened behind the white top.

"Fair enough. I still have a lot of learning to do, Little Shadow. But I know one thing…" he said, his tongue tracing the tingling line his fingers left.

I stiffened, not daring to move, my fingernails bloody at this point from how hard I was gripping the trunk of the palm tree.

"You're absolutely dripping for me."

I tightened my jaw, refusing to let his truth be confirmed. Instead, I gave a pathetic squeak that sounded like, "No, I'm not."

However, it had a question mark sound at the end of it, and the uncertainty was clearly audible. He jerked my knees apart, pressing his thigh in between my legs. I cursed, knowing his leg was fucking wet from me now.

He laughed.

The truth of my arousal glistened in the moonlight on his upper thigh. He grabbed my arm and spun me around so fast I didn't see it coming. My breath whooshed out of my lungs, making me feel dizzy.

"Ya know," he said almost conversationally.

Taking his foot, he knocked my feet out from underneath me, shredding my bathing suit bottom as I fell. I hit the sand on my knees, and then he was behind me, caging my wrists in his hands, cuffing me like a criminal. My addled, sexed-up brain was too over the edge to care. I needed it. I arched my back, ready to feel that monster length stretch me.

"I really hate liars," he said, his tone still lagging with lust but had a biting hint to it now.

I tried to turn my neck, but he gripped my hair firmly. Then, there was a sharp pain as strands were ripped.

"Tell me you're soaked for me," he demanded.

His ragged and angry pants told me his restraint was fraying with his need. My pussy wept. Liquid was running down my thighs, and I knew he could see it. He was so close to me. His heat burned me, sending flames across my skin.

"N-no," I managed to say, but my moan of need betrayed my words.

With a chuckle, he drove two fingers into my soaked pussy. Finger fucking me deep as he took my head and pushed my face down under the water.

Chapter 16

Lucius

y dick was impossibly hard right now. The damn
thing barely ever cooperated on the best of days, so
why the fuck was it a steel pipe for this infuriating woman. I
watched her struggle within the water and was curious how long she
could be under the surface. Her sex was clenched tightly around my
fingers, her slick heat searing me, and her lie was as evident as the
blood in her veins.

Her hands kept reaching back to scratch my hand with her
razor-sharp nails. The sting felt nice, and I chuckled at the drops of
blood forming. However, it was frustrating that she was warping my
tattoo. My very birth line. Moya Kotva or my blood. The insignia
of my fucked-up family in the red droplet-looking symbol covering
my hand.

I looked at my reflection in the water, my tanned skin and green
eyes glaring back at me. "Mirror, mirror on the wall. Who's the
sexiest killer of them all?"

Musing to myself, I noticed the little blonde was starting to
struggle less in my grip.

She was right on the cusp now. Those vital seconds in which the
meaning of life or death truly took hold of a person. I could end it,

snuff out her life like a candle flame, but there was something about this little killer that I couldn't stop thinking about.

She was…addictive.

Growling and hating this woman with my whole being, I pulled her up.

She was spluttering and gasping. Water streamed from her nose and mouth. Her makeup was all smeared, and her chest was rising so rapidly her tits popped out. My hands itched to bust open her bikini top.

I pulled out of her heat, making sure that she watched me lick each finger clean.

"You're right, Little Shadow…" I met her concrete glare of hatred with my own. "You are not wet at all."

She stood up, water dripping from her pale, long hair, leaving trails of clear crystals on her skin glistening like glitter in the moonlight. I wanted to lick them one by one. Her body was shaking. Her naked, creamy legs were like a baby deer's legs when they were first born. Then she wobbled and fell into a tree.

I pinned her down, her protests weak in her exhausted state. Pulling that fiery glare to meet my lips, I whispered in her ear. "You were wet before."

Her body stilled, her little panting gasps caught in my mouth.

"Now," I continued, licking the water dripping down her chest and letting my tongue trail over her swimsuit top, right over her tightening nipple.

"You're soaked."

She gasped in outrage, making me chuckle. A squeaking curse came out of that pretty mouth, and she shook her wavy tresses in my face like a damn dog.

"What the fuck?" I grumbled, wiping dirty river water from my eye.

She smirked at me, her gray-blue, granite-colored eyes swimming with rage.

"Now," she said, a smile lighting up her whole face. "You're soaked, too!"

It took me a second to grasp her sass, but she thought she could play with the devil and not get burned?

Smiling calmly, I flipped my hair back, ready to play another round. But, my Little Shadow did something I never expected.

She laughed.

Her entire face crinkled with pure joy, her body pretzeled into a full belly roll. She even had to catch herself on the tree to keep from falling onto the sandy ground.

I was speechless.

My brain was not able to function as the melodic song of her enjoyment laced around me like a glove. I thought she was beautiful when she killed, raged, and slept. This reaction, though…was otherworldly. It was an out-of-body experience, and I was captivated.

She was laughing because of me and at me.

I shouldn't be happy about this. I shouldn't be fighting a smile because of her joy. But here I was in awe, yet again, at this mesmerizing creature.

"What is your name?" I said, and the musical sound of her joy stopped. She stared at me with curious eyes.

"Jen," she said quickly. Too quickly. That was a lie.

I walked over to her. My arm was caging her but not touching her as she backed into a tree. She was using it like some sort of shield.

"Your real name is Maya Kayten," I pressed.

The tree created darkness for my Little Shadow, but the moonlight was shining on me. She studied me. Her eyes traced every line and scar. I was not going to take off my shirt. I didn't need her to see my past. But she could take her fill of the rest of me.

I gave her my best half-smile. "Like what you see?"

She rolled her eyes.

Brät.

"Fine," she said with a wistful sigh. "I'm Ember."

The spark that created an inferno—how accurate that was.

"Ember," I repeated, her name feeling nice on my lips.

She was so beautiful. Her wet blonde hair made her look like a mermaid. Her beautiful locks covered her breasts and ivory skin, which held the slightest pink blush to it. And god, those red lips with a Cupid's bow and her captivating blue-gray eyes…

She was beautiful.

She was mine.

I should kill her—right now and end this charade. It would get Markus, my father, and all the drug heads off my damn back.

Behead the princess and bring her crown to my city. Take back my castle, but…

"Why are you looking at me like that, Lucius?" she said, more innocent and shy than I'd ever heard her speak.

I blinked.

The thought of her blood on my hands—no. I couldn't. I won't.

"Because," I said, bracing myself for anything. "You're mine."

I dove at her, locking her against my body and spinning so she lay on top of me as I plunged us into the deep moonlit waters.

She gasped, unsure if I was going to try and drown her again. Letting go of her under the water, we surfaced and simply stared at each other. So, I just waded in the river beside her, my body heat rippling at her icy touch.

We were fire and ice, oil and water…cats and dogs. No, maybe not feline and canine, but we were like night and day or winter and summer.

We didn't fit.

Our lives didn't join. She was a shadow, and I was the ghost.

She was the killer of killers, and I slayed whomever I pleased. Nothing about us was remotely similar, yet the pull I had to her left me stuck as her captive.

The pull was an inescapable link, which I felt, but it was clear she did too. I could feel that she was just as helpless against it. The harder I fought to free myself from her, the more I needed her.

She looked at me. Those thick, black eyelashes wet, her golden hair creating a true crown around her head.

The princess just slayed the dragon because I was absolutely transfixed.

I needed her.

I would have her.

She.

Was.

Mine.

Gripping her luscious curves and pulling her to me, she moaned, her body so cool to the touch where I scorched her. I let my hand grip her breasts, sliding down to take a handful of her thick ass. My cock popped up, jabbing her in the stomach.

The water made us weightless, so I tried to tell myself, the feeling of floating was only because of the water. She reached over and gripped my dick in her small hand, running it from tip to base. The hiss I let out made her smile, and she did it again, faster. She was skilled and sure.

I growled, yanking her hand from me, pinning her hands behind her back, and holding her to me. We fell below the water, our breaths creating bubbles around our faces. I gripped her chin in my hands, bringing those dangerous lips to my own.

The coolness of the water did nothing to stop that heat from freezing me in place. Her tongue slipped into my mouth, beckoning and tasting. Her taste mingled with the salt of the water.

I wanted her so badly that it hurt.

Gripping her ass, I spread her legs with my knee, plunging my aching length into her in one swift thrust.

She whimpered. The sound created a cascade of bubbles all around us. Pulling her firmly onto my cock, I pulled us back to the surface. Sucking air back into my lungs was more a guttural cry of pleasure than for getting oxygen. Her slick pussy squeezed me, the water such a contrast to her warm, soft insides. She clung to me, coating me in her sweet honey-flavor.

I pinched her nipple, gripping her ass, making her ride me even harder and faster.

Her moans and scratching nails were the best thing I'd ever felt. Her hands reached for my shirt that was riding up, her fingers rubbing along the raised scars marring my back. I felt her gasp before I wrenched her hand away, pinning them on her ass.

My cock was twitching so hard, my balls so full, I needed a release.

"Fuck," I barked.

I knew I was nothing more than a crazed, possessed man, but I didn't care. This beautiful siren milked my cock and rocked her hips, riding the waves of the river and her own orgasm.

With one last moan, I came undone, marking her, making her mine.

It was too much and not enough.

I would never get enough.

"You are mine, Ember." Her head tipped forward, and she bit my shoulder. "Say it!"

I grabbed her chin, pressing my finger in her mouth, locking her teeth, and forcing her gaze to mine.

She moaned around my finger, undulating and shaking. Her breasts were pushed into my chest as she threw her head back, her hair floating around like ribbons of gold.

"I'm…" she gasped, her shaking was uncontrollable, adding to the friction and heady feel of her. "Yours."

Hearing those words—it did something to me, but what? I didn't know. A piece of me felt like it was cracking. I was a mirror that was sure to break. The thing was, I didn't know how to fix it, how to glue it back together.

After taking a bite of her—my glistening apple—I knew I would never be the same.

Snow White, indeed.

This dangerous woman had put a spell on me, and now, I was hers.

Chapter 17

A couple of days later, I received an anonymous note. The address on the note led Quinn and me to an abandoned warehouse. Sure enough, the stench of decaying rot and the swarms of flies told the tale of many animals that lost their lives here.

Judging by the skulls and hunks of humanoid-shaped rib cages littering the lines of the hallway, I had a feeling a different kind of animal was often brought here to be killed.

Humans.

The squelching sound under my boots made me gag. The Butcher could clean up his fucking mess. Geez.

Micah Quinn was always a diligent soldier. He always followed every order, had a kind smile when needed, or he was a ruthless man to deliver justice. Right now, though, facing these current circumstances, I'd laugh my ass off at his face. His Armani shirt was tucked over his nose, and his blue eyes were watering.

"It looks like whoever was here has cleared out," he said, a nasal tone to his voice. He was clearly holding his breath.

I inspected everything around me.

The boarded-up, broken windows and disgusting blood-soaked floor added to the awful ambiance. All of it just lay on the top. The epoxy finish was desperately trying to separate the death and rot from its beautiful shine.

It made it look like water, a reddish, black water.

The warehouse was corroded at the very base of the structure. The whole place had a slight tilt to it. Therefore, the red river pooled mostly down at the edge and dripped out of a busted window.

I shined my flashlight over to a boxed-in area. Cages, no bigger than a suitcase, were stacked neatly, row upon row.

Had they kept the animals here?

My question was quickly answered, and my heart sank as I approached the next corner. Naked, dismembered bodies lay haphazardly at the crook of the corner. Not giving a damn, I dove into the bodies. My heart was thundering so loud in my ears that it was like a bomb went off. There was just a buzz and whoosh of my blood pumping too fast throughout my body.

I could vaguely feel Quinn. His voice was a hazy mumble. All I could see were bodies. Heads were at different levels of decomposition. There were hair colors of all types: reds, blondes, blacks, and even neon colors. Textures were harder to depict. The matting of blood, what looked like oil, and a sticky clear liquid connected the hair on the severed heads together.

I couldn't see past my tears, my eyes blind as they tried to find their own reflection.

So many white, void, lifeless eyes stared back at me, and their spirits were like an icy hand on my body.

I felt them pulling, felt their bruising grip as they pulled me back.

Wait no. The hands wrapped around my chest weren't feminine and weren't trying to hurt me. I blinked. The feeling in my throat was a raspy, raw burn. Slowly, the watery buzz lifted from my ears, and Quinn's cries finally penetrated my consciousness.

"Ella," he yelled, taking hold of my face gently. His warm hands stroked my cheek. "Ella, come back. We don't know anything yet. Don't lose faith."

Faith never got me anything. I got myself here, not the Almighty God.

Me.

All that puppet master did was laugh at my misery.

"Please, sweetheart," Quinn continued, laying my numb body against his chest, our bodies soaked in the despair around us.

Cassie. My beautiful, naive sister. How could she be....

At the sound of a rattling cage, I felt my body snap back to reality, my limbs finally moveable, unfrozen. I jolted up, running toward the sound. My criminal analysis training was gone. Quinn shouted after me as I raced up a pair of corroded, cracking steps—each one groaning at my weight.

I lost my damn flashlight in the pile of limbs, so I could only use the light from the cracks in the boarded-up windows.

My heart stopped.

Inside an even smaller cage than I had seen before was a woman. She rattled the cage. Her body contorted. Her amber eyes looked like a zombie, glazed over and unseeing. Was she drugged?

Calling to Quinn I walked to the prisoner, the cage still rattling with her robotic smashing.

"Hi there," I said tentatively, showing my hands and walking slowly.

Quinn cursed as his eyes landed on the feeble girl.

"Was she abandoned? Or did someone bring her here?" I said to Quinn.

He shook his head and pulled his shirt off of him. I was going to hell for admiring the pounds of hard muscle on my partner right now. Shaking my head, I turned back to the person who had endured trauma.

"She's heavily drugged," I whispered, my gaze fixed on her unblinking eyes.

"We need to get her out of here," Quinn said, breaking the cage bars with just his strength.

He manipulated the bar so the lock simply fell off. The door creaked open, but the girl didn't move. She just kept smashing her hands into the same spot, but now was hitting the air. As gently as he could, Quinn grabbed the female, using his shirt to wrap around her naked and heavily bruised body.

The human part of me cried, and the cop part of me raged. Another part...wanted whoever tortured this poor woman to pay. Her fingernails were broken and bloody. She may be heavily drugged because she looked like a fighter. Her spirit, even in this world, was never broken. She humbled me to my bones.

Quinn wrapped her body more tightly in his shirt, cradling her head away from the gore on the bottom of the floor.

"You take her to the squad car," I told him, turning back to the Jenga puzzle staircase. "I need to make sure she's alone."

I could hear Quinn's protests. His assurances of calling this in, but I had to know. I had to look. My mind was racing with the hope and absolute terror that I might find Cassie here. As I approached the top of the staircase, the metal gave way, a huge slash cutting between my feet.

I tried to grab onto the wall, but it was no use. The unsteady metal cracked even more, and a groan like a ship rang out as it swung me sideways, smashing me against the wall. My body fell with the broken metal steps into darkness and rot.

Another soul to be kept prisoner of this butcher's shop.

I woke up, a painful sound of beeping in my ears. All I could make out was white: white walls, a white gown, white chairs, a white bed, and a white cover.

Snow freaking white.

The irony wasn't lost on me. I was in a hospital. That much was obvious. The annoying beep was some contraption stuck to my finger. A handsome nurse walked in. He had dark hair and green eyes, a strange smile playing on his lips as he approached me.

"Look at you," he said, a cheery tone in his voice, but it was off somehow. "We must call you sleeping beauty."

I cringed. I was no princess. And one had been taunting me for long enough.

"Where's my partner?" My voice sounded like gravel had been shoved down my throat.

He looked confused, grabbing my chart and reading over it.

"Sorry, you're all alone…" Scrolling down with his finger, he stopped with some unreadable expression in his eyes. "Ella, is it?"

I gave him a strange look. Did I know him? My brain was fried, and I felt like I swallowed a pound of hay.

"Interesting," he murmured, before grabbing something from my bag and walking out.

What the hell?

Since when did nurses steal from their patients?

Pulling off the annoying finger glove thing, I started to get up. My head whooshed, and I instantly saw black spots in my vision.

"Whoa!" I heard someone say. Strong arms caught me, laying me back in bed. I growled as those damn spots took over. A while later, I woke up again to that annoying beeping.

Groaning and swatting at the air, I grumbled, "Shut up."

A musical laughter sounded, and I opened my eyes to see Quinn. He cleaned up, and his pretty boy look had returned. This time, he was in his usual detective's get-up.

"Micah?" My voice sounded even worse now.

"Yeah. Hey, partner," he said, smiling and getting up to stand beside me. He reached onto the bed and squeezed my hand. His warm touch felt nice on my cool skin. "Sorry, I left you here for a bit. I was in another patient's room."

He looked sheepish, flustered, and even maybe tired. I looked at his hand on mine, noticing little red welt marks. He blushed at my gaze, removing his hand and running it through his blond hair. The smell of expensive spices wafted over to my nose.

I'm sure I smelled like a bag of sewage. Not only had I fallen off a damn staircase but into a pile of human remains.

Looking down at myself, I realized some poor sap had to give me a sponge bath. And I felt strangely uncomfortable about that. What if it was the moody nurse from before? Him seeing my body naked made me feel…flushed.

My hair on the otherhand had been haphazardly thrown up in a bun, with some half assed rinse.

"How's she doing?" I said, watching Quinn look almost shy.

"Oh," he said, blushing. "Yeah, she's…she's, uh…" he trailed off, tipping his hand back and forth in a "she's okay-ish" motion.

Honestly, it wouldn't be the truth to say she was okay. That woman had been through hell and made it out alive. But that just meant her body survived. It wouldn't be known for a while if her mind did.

"She was tortured for months," he said. His tone was sad, his eyes almost haunted. I knew this brought up memories of his sister. I reached my hand over to pat his big, burly chest.

He looked up, and his blue eyes had a smile in them, but the pain was clear as day. He was definitely thinking about his little sister. What she must have suffered. Death was a mercy for her in the end.

"She's been burned." he trailed on, absent in how he spoke.

"Raped." he continued, that sad tone nearly a whisper. "Beaten and cut."

I cringed. Jesus, I really hoped she could find a way to live a normal life.

"Her bones had been broken and rehealed incorrectly…" I realized he was spitting out facts that were not just about the patient but facts from the coroner's report for his seventeen-year-old sister.

Tears were freely streaming down his face, his beautiful, solid, and protective walls broken. The very soldier he was, and he was shattering before me. Wincing at the damned pain from my body, I ignored it, spinning my body to embrace him. He was a tortured soul, my partner, and my friend.

"Her name is Ivy. Not Penelope…she's not Pen—" A sob he tried desperately to hide had cut off his words.

His body shook as he finally embraced me back.

My heart broke. I wanted so badly to help him.

"Tell me about Ivy," I said, trying to get him out of his head. "What is she like? Have the drugs worn off?"

It worked. He pulled back from the hug, a slight smile pulling at his lips.

"She's the most full-of-life person I've met with all she's been through, but she is still a fighter."

"Is that fighting spirit what gave you those love marks?" I teased, pointing to his hand.

"Very funny…she's not…I wouldn't." He blushed.

"I know, I'm only teasing," I said.

"She is an adamant young lady, though," he said with a chuckle.

I wondered more about Ivy. How could someone still be a person after that? I certainly broke in two with my own trauma as a teenager. One of the reasons Quinn and I had such a close bond was that I very well could have ended up like Penelope or Ivy. It had been chance or maybe dumb luck that I'd gotten out of there.

"I know you took them! Give them back. Okay, then I'll dig them out of you."
His clown-like voice echoed in my ears, the deranged laughter causing nausea to
bubble in my throat. I shivered at the memory of his cold hands carving into my
skin like a zombie.

Quinn noticed my face and got up to grab me some water.

"Sorry, Ella. I should let you sleep," he said, shaking his head and fussing with his beard. It looked longer than usual. "They're letting you out later. You have some bruises and a few scrapes, but otherwise, you're okay, thank god."

I pondered that. I would be happy to be free of this white prison. I hated hospitals, everything from the old people, the bleach smell, the television static, and the flashes of blue from all the nurses running around. Not to mention all the beeping. It was all too much for me.

"I'll see you back at the station," I said, trying to smile. "Oh, and Quinn? Have my nurse changed."

Closing the door behind me, I breathed a sigh of relief. My jailbreak was successful. I walked over to her. The small framed girl lying in the bed that dwarfed her...she was maybe five feet, if that. She had little to no weight on her, but not by her own choosing. I couldn't imagine the things she'd eaten to survive. But her long black hair was still quite beautiful. It was washed up and curled like springs at her sides.

She was quiet, and I thought she was sleeping. Turning back, I made my way back to the door.

"I recognize you," she said, a thick accent popped out...maybe Russian? I froze, turning back around sheepishly and planting my busted ass on the chair beside her.

"Hi. Yes," I greeted her. "I'm Ella. You met my partner earlier...I was the one to find you at that..." I let my words trail off. The only fitting name for that horrid place was a slaughterhouse.

"I know," she said curtly, her amber eyes now clear and I could see a very light green around the outside.

"You're beautiful," I blurted out, feeling like a dumbass when she flinched. She was nearly every shade of yellow and purple from the bruises coating her head to toe. And she was missing parts of her skin in places. Her cheeks were sunken in, and her ribs poked out of her little hospital gown.

"I guess it feels good to hear when it's not from those monsters," she said at last.

I made a mental note that she'd used the word 'monsters.' That meant multiple people did this to her. And the others who were still and forever stuck in that horrible place.

Chapter 18

Ember

Tracking Lucius, I had to be careful. He was always finding me. Always the predator. I was going to make him feel how it felt to be the prey for once. Keeping to the shadows, I pulled my black mask firmly above my nose. The only thing visible were my eyes.

"Come out, come out, little prince."

I mused to myself, focusing the binoculars at the warehouse. Lucius seemed angry. It looked like he was screaming at some man. His rage was rolling off him in waves. He smacked the guy across the face. The crack was loud enough to hear it from where I hid in the distance. The echo was like a shot in the air.

The impact brought the man to the ground. I flipped open my laptop, adjusting the small device in my hand. I watched on the screen as the little bars began to rise.

"Who the fucking hell do you think you are?" Lucius screamed, the device picking up his murderous rage.

The other guy sputtered blood on the ground.

"It was necessary," he pleaded, raising his hands in surrender.

Lucius looked absolutely savage, standing over him, "Putting my flesh and blood in a fucking cage for your own power is not a necessity."

Cranking the volume up, I continued to listen.

"You don't understand. Your father would have given her the command. We all would be under her rule. She's the eldest. I did you a favor."

The savage beast of a man roared. Pain and fiery bouncing off my computer screen and through the air around me.

"I went to that hospital. I was checking on something and imagine my surprise to see my fucking sister chatting to a cop that's asking who tortured and mutilated her."

His voice was calm now. A dead whisper as he looked in the eyes of the terrified guy on the ground.

"Were you the one to take my sister from her bed? Beat and torture her? Brand and violate her body for nearly a year?"

As Lucius spoke, he dug in the dirt with a metal-looking object. I guessed a shovel. The guy on the ground was sobbing—a wet puddle pooling around him.

"Please," the man cried.

I watched as Lucius continued to dig, sweat dripping from his body, soaking his shirt and hair. The hole was getting deeper and deeper.

"I did it for you!"

Lucius finished his work, hopped out of it, and back to the soiled, sobbing man.

"Wrong. Answer."

Those two words flipped a switch. I could see the fire build inside him, and the second it consumed his soul. Walking over to the whimpering torturer, he grabbed him by the arm...and ripped it clean off his body.

The guy screamed, blood squirting from the wound. With a growl, Lucius smiled. "No, no. Not that easily, dear cousin."

Cousin? This man was related to him?

Captivated, I continued to watch as Lucius seared his old-fashioned lighter to his skin. The wound was cauterized and stopped the bleeding. He took the loose arm, tossed it in the hole, and grabbed the other, twisting and grunting as it was pulled from his body.

This continued—severing and ripping off body parts. The man was alive while watching himself be torn apart. He wasn't just a dark prince.

He was a beast.

The precision it took to keep this man alive to meter out his death was overly gruesome, extremely passionate, and entirely too real. He truly was my equal.

"Now," he told the lump with no legs, arms, or tongue. "I'm going to bring her here, and I'm going to let her watch as the pathetic waste who was sworn to protect her but broke her instead be destroyed bit by bit."

Chapter 19

Lucius

*H*aving only one goal in mind and no time to play, I stalked the halls of the Strong Memorial Hospital. The stench of mothballs and bleach tickled my nose.

I came to my sister's room. She had a fucking pretty boy cop blocking her door.

For fucking real. Go be a hero somewhere else.

I was on a time crunch. Markus could die from infection in his stink of a warehouse. I didn't even have to go in to smell the rot.

The thought of my sister living in that…made my blood boil.

I didn't want to make a scene by killing this pretty boy, and so I dipped into the supply closet, throwing on a pair of scrubs and a white coat. The blood on my hands and face surprisingly fit in well around here.

Walking up to the pretty boy cop, I plastered on a smile.

"Hi, how's our patient doing?" I mimicked the annoying fake-ass tone of all the real doctors in this place.

The cop looked at me, suspicion evident in his eyes.

"Who are you?" he said, his tone grouchy, authoritative.

The dude sounded like a roid-rager. Eyeing him, he looked like one too. He had a good five inches on me. I wasn't GQ tall. My dick took most of my height. I was a nice five feet, ten inches. Tall enough to headbutt large assholes like this in the nuts and short enough to give perfect tongue fucking while piloting my heli. Tall shit stains were overrated.

"The patient is the kidnapped woman, right?" I said, ignoring him and trying to look past his bulky ass to see through the window. I couldn't, and the meathead blocked my view even more.

"Not sure, Doc," he said. "You tell me."

I glared at him. He in no way would take me down. I threw dicks like him over my shoulder daily.

"All right, creatine, calm your balls."

He returned my glare. "Where's your ID?"

It wasn't a question.

Smiling, I reached down to my pocket, his gaze following, his body leaning over slightly.

"Here it is," I said, waiting for him to lean down a little more.

My knee made contact with his face, his muscular form falling with a huge thud.

Smirking, I wiped off my hand on his expensive shirt and opened the door to the room.

Feeling anxious and a little lost, I hid behind the curtain. I didn't hear any noise. It was early morning, after all. It was probably around two a.m. or so.

I hadn't seen my sister in three years, and she'd been missing for one of those years.

The last time I saw my happy, sassy sister was in Russia at the ballroom studio. It was a week before I had left. The scars of that day's lashing had seared pain in my back with a memory I'd prefer to forget.

Father had watched me perform a tango with Sasha. I had practiced for hours. I was forcing myself to replay the steps over and over until I moved without telling my body to do so but purely off the beat of the music.

My sister was in the front row. Her smiling face cheered me on as Sasha and I swirled around the dance floor. I had won. The medal felt heavy on my neck. I remembered the feeling of the weight of the trophy and how I had always imagined it being heavier when I was growing up.

But then screams started. My father slammed into my sister, covering her from the spray of bullets, screaming at me to shield our mother.

My feet were unable to move, and I swore she was moving in slow motion, watching my innocent mother as she ran to me. She wanted to cover me when I should have protected her. Her white dress, dark wavy hair, and smiling face were a pure reflection of my own features…then there was so much blood.

Crimson lines and puddles were everywhere from the bullets—they had painted her red. Her body fell onto the ground at my feet, and my father and sister screamed in horror. More people fell as they, too, were painted with red. A black, maroon pool began splashing until a tide of it swallowed my ankles, and I was sure I was going to drown.

Bang.

Bang.

Bang.

Shots just kept coming, and my ears rang as my father shot the men who shot my mother—every single one of them.

To this day, his agonized roars still echoed in my ears. The way he cradled my mother's head and the way his rage and torment carried throughout our family became my burden. That metaphorical lance had sliced my back and my blood, which had joined that of the fallen.

I had left that night, flying off to America. I learned how to be a hunter and protect those I loved. Finally, I learned to kill. I didn't tell a soul. My father sent his lackeys, eventually finding me in New York, but by that time, I had been a ghost long enough to rebuild myself and create a home.

In America, I wasn't just the son of Moya Kotva, the mafia's leader. I was Lucius Vasiliev. I didn't want to look at my sister and see that weak, pathetic man I'd left behind so long ago in the reflection of her eyes.

"Who is there?" A small voice said—a feminine Russian voice. So much like my mother, it brought tears to my eyes.

"Privyet…It's me, Eilizaveta," I said, my voice breaking.

"You're Bratva?"

Seeing my sister was even more painful than I could have ever imagined. Her body was so broken and marred. Her torture on the outside was not even close to what they'd done to her soul.

I felt my chest tighten. Markus's words in my ear, "I did it for you. So you have the power!"

My sister was put through true hell because of me.

"Do not say that name," she said numbly. "I am Ivy now. The girl Eilizaveta was taken by monsters and destroyed."

A tear slipped free of my face. It landed on her dark hair.

"I missed you, sestra. I searched for you…I never thought our Kotva would do this—"

She stopped my rambling. Her frail hand came up to wipe at my cheek. Not realizing I had tears flowing down my face like a fucking baby.

Her hand was so soft. So much like my mother's, the tears kept streaming down my stupid face, and I couldn't stop them.

Eilizaveta, no Ivy now, cradled me in her arms, holding my head and soothing me by running her fingers through my hair.

"Ya tebya lyublyu," she murmured, singing the lullaby our mother always did.

"I love you too."

Brushing off my tears and trying to get a grip, I remembered the time crunch for Markus, and I didn't want her to miss his death.

"Sestra," I said, making sure to look in her golden eyes. They were a carbon copy of our father's, and it was painful to do so, but I reminded myself this was Eili.

"I have our cousin. The traitor."

Her eyes lit up, a spark igniting and making them. They looked like molten lava. "Take me to him," she demanded, her frail body swinging over the side.

"I will," I promised. "But then I have to bring you back." I looked out the window to her room. The pretty boy cop was still asleep. "Your guard dog will bite me if I don't."

She smacked my arm, her eyes rolled, and I thought her cheeks looked rosier. It could be the exertion from the long year she had.

"The Porthos aren't bad," she shrugged, and that was all I was going to get.

Going over and slipping on a nice red dress, she smiled. My sister always was a debutant. Her being able to have simple things again, like pretty dresses, made me smile.

"A pretty cop lady gave it to me," she said, smiling.

I didn't like cops, but I guess this one was okay.

"Get a paper and pen, too, brät," she ordered.

Confused, I said, "Why?"

"Because he needs to tell you where he put the other girl before I end him."

Chapter 20

Ella

I smiled. Quinn seemed really happy. He said the prisoner from the warehouse was a lot happier. Her resilience astounded me.

"You seem pretty happy yourself there, detective." I teased. I could practically see his blush through the phone.

"Yes, well, it's nice seeing a civilian bounce back," he huffed.

I smiled wider. "Yes, of course. Especially a beautiful Russian model one."

"Ella," he chided. "Stop playing Cupid."

I was about to comment on another dumb joke. But then he got serious. "I am worried someone is after her. Maybe the people who tortured and kidnapped her. I'm not sure, but I woke up in a chair. I never sleep on the job. I always protect my mark."

I frowned. That was a scary thought, but Quinn was so tired it was possible he might have fallen asleep. I didn't say as much. Instead, I asked if he wanted to grab some ice cream or something.

"I can't. Sorry. I really need to keep an eye on Ivy."

I nodded, agreeing.

"Okay?" he said, concern lacing his gruff tone. "I would if I could, Elle, but I just have a weird feeling."

I realized I hadn't spoken and nodded to a phone like a dumb-ass, so I said aloud this time. "Yes, I completely understand. You're a good man, Micah. Penelope would be proud of who you are."

He was quiet for so long that I thought he'd hung up. But then, I heard him barely whisper, "Maybe."

There was so much pain and hope in one word.

I felt that deep in my soul.

The emotions ran wildly through my heart as we waited for forensics to get back to us regarding IDs for the multiple victims in that slaughterhouse. My world teetered with the blinding hope that Cassie wasn't among them.

I held my stomach. The ache set deep, my nerves and pain swirling in my blood like poison.

"Has anyone claimed her yet? A partner? Family?" I said, forcing myself to breathe through this awful panic. Shutting down the emotions that wouldn't bring Cassie back, I held onto the ones that would.

"No," he said. I could hear papers flipping around as he shuffled for something. A slight 'a-ha,' and he drawled. "She spoke to a psychologist at ten am this morning. It says on her charts she referred to losing her parents when she was little and never having married. And not having any other family," he read.

I frowned. Geez, this girl went through hell, survived, and now she was alone in this world? How the fates were cruel.

"Okay, well, maybe we can track down friends she may have known. She has such a thick Russian accent. Was she kidnapped from there and brought to the States?"

Quinn was silent, more shuffling and then a groan.

"She wouldn't say. Her statement just says she was sleeping, and they took her."

I pondered that. "Plural. They. Whoever was behind this—it had to be two or more people."

I didn't mention that she said the same last night when I visited her right before being discharged. My body was banged up, but as opposed to usual, I didn't notice much difference. The stairs hadn't been all that high. I was more likely to die from a disease of getting scraped in that fungus-infested grave site than the fall itself.

"I agree. I have spoken with her myself," he admitted. That must have been off-book because he'd been off duty since getting her from that horror.

"Did you stay at the hospital?" I said, realizing that he had to have been there a while to collect all that data.

There was a beat of silence and then a long sigh. "Yeah, I just wanted to make sure she was okay. Had someone familiar around for a bit."

Quinn had to have been hurting badly from this, his sister's treatment and death at the forefront of his memory. And yet he was still being the kind man he was, making sure that a scared woman had a friend.

God, they should make medals for the guy. I certainly was no saint. That was for sure. I mean I became a criminal analyst because I couldn't deal with what happened to me. I needed to find every bad man and save every seventeen-year-old girl from the same fate.

"Ella," he said, a serious note to his tone. "Did something like that happen to you?"

I blinked. Micah Quinn had read my file.

"Uh, no. Nothing like Ivy. I was kidnapped at a friend's place... when I was walking back home, some tweakers knocked me out and threw me in a trunk."

My heart rate picked up, and my mind went all fuzzy. It was like static, trying to find a channel. "I don't remember much at all, to be honest..." I admitted.

My heartbeat thrummed wildly in my ears. I didn't remember

anything past being shoved in a trunk. I obviously got away some-how, but....

Quinn was silent, his own mind's cruelty bogging him down.

"I'm so sorry, Ella. You're very strong."

"I think it killed my dad," I blurted. "He was never the same after that. And honestly, I felt like a stranger when I came home. I had moved out later that year, putting all my focus on becoming a CA."

Quinn murmured all the right things. The way my dad loved me, the way he never would have judged me. But I couldn't know for sure. My dad was gone.

Arriving at the hospital, I was greeted by a kind receptionist. Her mousy face and slim neck made her look like a fascinating creature. Actually, she kind of looked like a painting.

"Hi there," she said—a southern accent prominent. She was a classic Southern belle.

"How do I get to room two-one-one, please."

"Oh, that's the room that handsome detective visits. He has barely left her side," she said with a dreamy sigh. Quinn was always leaving girls wistful in his wake.

"Thank you," I said and walked to the gift shop.

I didn't know what was a good gift to give. What did you give to someone that says, 'I'm so happy a bunch of torturing rapists did not murder you for nearly a year.' Well, those were the details written on the reports.

A fluffy oversized teddy bear?

No, that would make her feel suffocated.

What about candy hearts?

No, she needed to eat soft foods and slowly adjust back to normal.

A blade to slice up her enemies?

I blinked—the thought surfaced like an alien. Shaking my head, I decided on a balloon and flowers. She could pop it if she didn't want it, but the flowers would smell nice and give her that sense of fresh air she reveled in last night.

Quinn greeted me, an uncomfortable-looking chair laid next to the wall by her door entryway.

"You should go home and rest," I scolded him, seeing the thick black bags under his head and a bruise-like mark on his forehead. "Are you all right?" I said, concerned at why he'd have a big bruise forming there.

He touched the foreign mark, blowing me off and waving his hand. "I'm fine, Ella. Just clocked myself somehow. I fell asleep on duty. I deserve worse."

I frowned. I didn't know why he was punishing himself...literally.

"I got her, Quinn," I stated, gently squeezing his arm. "Go home, Micah. Just for a little while. Let yourself sleep."

Micah looked around, his eyes settling on that chair.

I wagged my finger, giving it a shove with my foot. It scraped on the hospital floor and made us both cringe.

"No, no." I chastised. "You need to go to bed for real."

Groaning and worrying his beard, he looked through the window at the patient. Her eyes met his, and they shared some moments I felt awkward witnessing. It felt private, like it was for their eyes only.

"Fine," he grumbled. "I'll book a suite next door at the Marriott. I'm not going back to my place it's too far."

I refused to try to tell this stubborn ox that nine minutes to get to his place wasn't that far away. So, instead, I hugged him.

Ivy was a very quiet girl. She thanked me for the flowers and stared curiously at the balloon with the words "It's a girl" written on it. They didn't have anything else, so she mostly just stared out the window with a vacant look in her pretty bronze-colored eyes.

"So," I said, wincing at my own voice at how loud it seemed compared to the normal hospital bustling.

"You and Quinn seem to be getting along."

A ghost of a smile played on her lips.

"The detective is…he is different."

I got that. And I agreed. Even by normal standards Quinn was a golden boy, a decorated soldier, and smart as hell law enforcement. "Yeah, he's pretty great." I said.

Ivy ran her fingertips along the side of an apple, the waxy skin imprinting with her touch. "I cannot eat this yet," she said, twirling it in her small hands.

"But I can enjoy its beauty."

I stared at the apple—the glossy coating shining from the sunlight outside the window. I pondered how an apple would be a source of joy to look at and touch. So many sensations depraved for so long, only knowing pain, fear, and survival.

"You'll be able to eat it soon," I said. Not knowing medically when exactly she could get off the mushy food exactly but feeling like that hope was important to assure in her. She chuckled. The sound lilted, musical.

"Your lies are krasivvy." I pondered that. My lies are what? Stupid? Weird? Mean? "Beautiful," she repeated in English.

I smiled at her, preparing to say it wasn't a lie, but my phone buzzed. Giving Ivy an apologetic look, I walked toward the hallway and answered. "This is Ella."

Ally's voice was on the other line.

"Hey, Ella," she said. Her matter-of-fact, no-bullshit tone was in full swing.

"What did you find?" I said, deciding against small talk. She was silent for a minute.

"Well, we're still trying to ID the victims. We know two-hundred and thirty-four people were killed. This is going back years. Some of the decomposition levels are well within the five to six-year range. We're analyzing the brain matter and retinal fluids as best—"

I cringed. I knew about all that stuff…blood and guts, but it didn't mean I loved hearing about it. I had washed my hair about forty-five times, but still, the pale blonde strands were tinted a permanent red.

"And so there was another discovery at the scene that really needs attention."

I stopped, honing into whatever she was about to say.

"Did you find Cassie?" I said both, hoping for a 'Yes we did' and 'No we didn't.'

Ally sighed. "No, your sister and her DNA have not matched any of the victims. The ones we're still sorting through have a decomposition level of much older than when she went missing. It's likely she is not in that warehouse."

I audibly sighed, my heart squeezing with that dreaded hope. A bubble I couldn't pop, my own sanity held in the small containment.

"But we did find something interesting," she continued. "There was fresh blood at the scene," she corrected. I pondered that. Worried we missed a girl. "It was male."

Now, I was confused.

Looking over to Ivy, I said, "Were males also being held prisoner at that place?"

Ivy shook her dark brown head. "No. Males were monsters."

I frowned.

"The survivor from there says no males were kept. That they were the abusers." Ally clicked her tongue. "Interesting," she said, and her fingers went clicking away on a computer.

"Do you think it could be one of the attackers?" I said, the continued clacking of her keyboard overpowering my voice.

"You said the survivor? What is the name of the person?"

"I'm not sure she just goes by Ivy," I whispered, turning my back away from her.

"I'm downloading her files now," she informed me.

Clack, clack, clack, clip, clack.

Ugh…

"Okay, so it doesn't say much as far as any information, but—" She stopped, the silence stretching. "Oh…that is interesting."

Annoyed, I blew a strand of hair from my face.

"Ally? What's interesting?"

She continued to type. Her "Hmm" and "Oh, I see" responses drummed in my ear.

"Ally!" I barked.

The clacking stopped. "Ella, are you with the patient now?"

Confused, I looked over to Ivy and nodded. "Yes, why?"

Ally took a deep breath. "The blood samples collected at the scene were from outside. A male dismembered and likely tortured was found in a hand-dug hole. The soil had recently been disturbed, and it's been concluded that the DNA from your patient and the victim from the scene most recently perishing there have similar infrastructures in the RNA strands of the biological genesis genes."

I blinked, trying to piece together her nerd-talk.

Ally did it for me. "In other words, the patient you're with right now, Ella, is related to the man who was killed."

Chapter 21

Sitting in my tent, I began writing down everything that had been happening lately.

Randall came up to my tent. He looked a bit skittish. I hadn't spoken to him since our huge fight that night. He didn't want to be involved in my business, which was fine. But why was he walking up to me now, looking like the devil was chasing him?

"I just wanted to thank you. For ya know, everything," he said, his voice a bit shaky.

I waved my hand.

"It was nothing."

These people deserved more than a few credit cards could get them. A bunch of the younger members, who had slept all the time and I thought were dumb as rocks, had actually moved out and gotten jobs. They used the thousand to put up rent in an apartment nearby. They pooled it together and were now roommates. It made sense that they would feel safe to stick together.

The older, grumpy members stayed behind. The sick ones who sneezed all the damn time went off to the hospital, using the money to get the proper care they needed. The really smart tech wiz left.

Maybe he'd end up running a company. It was pretty cool what a simple thousand could do for some people.

The little homeless community was now thinned out to just seven people, including Randall and me.

"You can act like you don't care." Randall continued. His demeanor was more bashful, not at all his happy self. "But it meant a lot to me. Thank you, Ember."

He bent down and pulled me into an awkward hug.

Feeling strange, I patted him on the back and said, "It's nothing anyone else wouldn't have done. Any decent person anyway."

I laughed despite myself. I wasn't decent at the best of times, really. But the homeless people deserved so much.

"Yeah, maybe, " he said, that haunted gaze lingering around. Shaking himself, he finally said, "Well, thanks. I'll see ya around."

Feeling odd about that whole encounter, I tried to brush it off, but it felt like bugs were crawling over me.

I had to hurry. If I was going to catch Lucius and see what the ever-loving fuck he was up to, I was going to have to think on my feet. I had watched him and that frail girl that night. He had held her with a delicate hand. One that made me feel a spike of jealousy. But that was stupid.

I hated this man....didn't I?

Maybe, but the way he was so calm with her, how he had gently set her on a lawn chair, bringing that lump of a man to her who was surprisingly still alive…I kept wondering if the girl knew him.

She was beautiful, even while looking very bruised and malnourished. She had very pretty brown hair. It was very dark but not black. She was short. Lucius had a good ten inches on her. He wasn't some giant. His height was nice. It was the perfect height for when he held my face to his, kissing me deeply…

I let that thought trail off. My hands flushed as I stared at my pen and paper. I had tried to recreate the strange symbol I'd seen on that guy's mouth before that girl had killed him. She shredded his torso to ribbons. In fact, she didn't stop until her nails cracked. Even his ribcage had been opened, and his heart had been out from his chest.

Whatever that guy did to her, the kill was personal. My own brutality was not based on excessive torture or wasted energy. The word ripper bounced around in my head—the ultimate cartel leader. So many had thrown the name at me, saying they didn't know who this killer was. All anyone knew was that if I wanted to look for the boss, then I needed to look for The Ripper.

Was it possible that The Ripper was this frail-looking female?

I replayed the image in my head. How calm and gentle Lucius was with her. How sweet and uncharacteristically childlike around her. Was she related to him? Was he protecting her?

If she was, in fact, The Ripper, then I needed to find her. And Lucius was not going to like it. I always knew that we'd end up fighting someday. The draw we had was undeniable, but the reality of our worlds being connected…no.

When fire and ice could co-exist, then maybe.

There was no way he would give me that girl without a fight to the death. His kindness and careful movements around her made that evident.

So it was time.

Time to end this.

Once and for all.

I arrived at the hangar. The helicopter was tan with black markings, sleek-looking just like its owner. In scrawled handwriting on the side of it, the name read, "Kotva Vasiliev."

This was the helicopter that Lucius spoke about that night. The one he said he'd take the girl in and find whatever they were seeking. Pulling the symbol from my pocket, I traced the weird edges with my fingertips. Putting it away, I grabbed the helicopter manual and read about the engines.

Taking my knife, I sliced a wire from the control panel and closed it up. The sound of a large metal cranking had me cursing. The door to the hangar was opening. Not wanting to lose the element of surprise, I opened the helicopter door and dove into the back. There was a little hatch there, and I hid inside it.

I could hear mumbled voices: Lucius, his guards, and a female.

Bingo!

The voices stopped when they got to the helicopter. The hatch door was cracked open, and I wasn't able to close it fully.

Damnit.

"Reggie, did you leave my heli open?" Lucius said, his voice suspicious.

Reggie mumbled something like he didn't think so, and Lucius laughed, popping it open fully. Hidden in the hatch, I held my breath. Lucius's hot stare burned through me.

"Change of plans boys. You ride separately. Take the money," he said.

Fuck! Did he see me?

"I'm going to take Eili myself. We'll meet you at the coordinates." His tone didn't leave room for argument. His soldiers simply walked away, their footsteps echoing as they went off into the distance.

The helicopter shook, the big bad serial killer hopping into the pilot's seat. Then, the aircraft barely bounced as he loaded up his passenger.

"Reggie did my preflight check earlier. We're cleared," he said to the girl, but there was no response in return.

I turned my gaze to the control panel, knowing the wire had been sliced.

How the fuck was this going to go.

Chapter 22

Lucius

iring up the helicopter, I watched my sister hang on frantically to the top edge. She was terrified—her normal tan complexion was pure white.

"Eili, it's okay," I offered, reaching over and squeezing her knee. "I'm here, and I will make sure no one ever fucking touches you again."

She shivered at the rage in my voice but nodded. My promise, my blood.

"Who is this girl?" I said, not knowing a fucking thing on the rando. "I'm flying my ass to Boston to get—"

"Markus…" she stopped, flinching at even the sound of his name. It broke my heart to see my fiery sister so…muted.

"He took a girl to the warehouse," she said.

I furrowed my brows, not wanting to think of that place and the horror it held for my sister.

"I don't know her name, but she managed to escape him," she continued. I was intrigued. My sister was a fucking fighter. She had been held captive for so long because of their consistency in drugging her.

She fidgeted, picking at the skin on her nail. This detoxing cold turkey was her idea, and it was so painful to watch.

"I don't remember much. I was being used in another room," she said. My jaw clenched so hard I felt my teeth nearly crack.

"I could hear a fight. The girl ran. She was free."

I knew there was more to it, or we wouldn't be in the air now.

"But?" I countered.

"But," she said, her voice now wavering. "Stupid girl came back for me."

I ran my hand along my five o'clock shadow, even my soulless heart feeling bad for the girl with a pure heart.

Regretfully, I said, "What happened?"

Eili turned away, her dark brown hair with the shimmer coming back. It was the only thing I could see.

"I don't know," she said to the air. "I just know Markus said she'd be a gift..." She turned back around, and her golden eyes pierced my soul. The gold look spilled away to a hazy green. "For you, Lucius."

I frowned. "What?"

"Markus said, 'The girl was a gift for you.' "

I blinked. The brown-haired girl. The escort. The one Markus brought to the club. He had said that.

"I declined," I said.

She glared at me. "Another's body is not yours to decline, Bratva!"

I kept my mouth shut. There wasn't anything I could say to that.

"Okay, well, we're almost ther—" An alarm sounded, the blaring noise filling up the space.

Smoke started to billow from the hood, and it made my sister cough. Swatting smoke from my face, I looked for a place that was clear to land. There was not going to be much of a damn choice.

A clearing in a goddamn cow field was the only option. The

helicopter started to spin as I pulled back the cyclic controls and prepared for what I knew would be a hard landing. Smashing the skids on the ground and losing one, I watched, terrified, as the blade caught the grass, causing the helicopter to flip over. The blade section went flying, and so did we.

I wrapped my body around my sister, holding on to her like bubble wrap.

I was thrown onto my back. The livestock fleed the area, huddling up against a wooden fence. Damn, the helicopter could have at least made a free burger or two, but no, the cows were just mocking us as we lay in their shit.

Taking a look at my aircraft, I cringed. It wasn't on fire, but it was ruined.

Feeling a mix of disgust, worry, and a fuck ton of pain, I tested my arms. My sister seemed unharmed. She was lying on my chest, her petite body as light as a feather. Snow White wasn't a feather. She was a goddamn weapon. When I held her, I felt every curve in my hands.

"Are you okay?"

My sister rose to her feet, surveying the whole lot of fucking nowhere. I knew I was a shit-talker, but I spat out actual shit this time. Vomiting, I flipped off the mound of beef and yanked off my shirt.

My sister's eyes snapped to my back—the scars left by my father's pain. Fuck. I wasn't thinking. I just wanted something not covered in shit. Eili gasped. The notion that she was an array of all colors from bruising and because she was reacting this way to my scars was ridiculous.

I turned my gaze away from her.

"Papa?" she said, running her light fingertips over the marred pink flesh.

I just nodded.

"It was the day Mama died," I said, my voice numb, cold, and broken.

"Lucius, I am so sorry." Her eyes welled with tears.

"Don't be," I gently wiped her tears with my thumb. "I learned what it meant to pay in blood that night."

Eili frowned and shook her head.

"No, Lucius. We were young. Papa shouldn't have put that on your shoulders. You were only fifteen."

I knew this, but I still couldn't let it go. I should have protected our mother.

"I just froze," I admitted in defeat.

"When it mattered the most, I fucking froze, and now the only innocent blood in our family is on my hands. She's gone."

"Mama would be proud of you, Lucius."

Foreign tears stung the corner of my eyes, and I aggressively wiped at them. Eili pulled my arm, my vision so blurry that I couldn't see, so I let her lead the way. We arrived at a farmhouse. The old cottage looked homey, and the people who answered even more so. It was rare to see the true kindness that lived in their eyes.

Gertrude and Hank were their names, and they immediately took us in and began helping us.

"Oh, you poor dears," Gertrude crooned, grabbing a plate of cookies and shoving them toward us. I grabbed half the plate, and Eili took one and picked at the corners.

"We're so glad you're unharmed," Hank said, his gruff voice aged with hard work and dedication to his farmland.

Not long after, they allowed us to take a shower and eat a proper meal. I would have personally starved to death over not showering. I was going to mail them fifty thousand dollars in an anonymous check when I got back to Rochester. Half of that probably needed to be used on more shampoo.

· · ·

"Absolutely not," Gertrude said, her old hand wagging at me in disbelief. "You are not riding with some stranger named Uber. You will stay here tonight, and Hank will take you where you were headed in that flying death machine," she said, her voice not leaving room for discussion.

I sighed, tucked my tail like the whipped dog I was, and obeyed.

"You get some sleep, Eili," I said, grabbing a coat Hank let me borrow from the bed.

She looked at me suspiciously. "What about you?"

I shrugged. "I'm going to take a look at the helio," I said. "Whatever the fuck is left of it, that is."

Eili argued, but ultimately, her exhaustion got the best of her. She kissed me on the cheek, making me bend down like a pretzel to do so, and let me leave.

The cow field smelled as much like a wad of shit as before. The stench not being better in the night air.

Walking to the helicopter, I saw pieces thrown all around the field. Some cows had used them as seats, which made me laugh. So much for giving a shit about an alien invasion. These fuckers would just sit on them.

Sighing, I walked around the cabin door. The back hatch was slightly ajar, and strands of pale blonde hair were sticking out.

What the fuck?

Walking closer, I opened the hatch and jumped back. Passed the fuck out in her very own little hidy-hole, a little stow away was sleeping. Unharmed and unbothered.

What the fuck?

Did she not notice we fucking crashed?

Speaking of, I walked to the control panel, my eyes homing in on the wire that was nearly severed in two.

Glaring at the sleeping beauty, I saw a barn on the side of the cottage. Slinging the woman who slept like the fucking dead over my shoulder, I walked to the barn.

Flopping her like a bale of hay, I said, "Wakey, wakey, princess."

She didn't budge.

Hmm, maybe she did get hurt by the fall after all? I began scanning her for injuries. Running my hand over her arm, checking for any blemishes, I barely felt her stir. That was until her elbow went flying into my face.

Smashing into the ground, I cursed.

"What the fuck?"

She screamed. She looked truly terrified, haunted, even like she was somewhere else. She was backing up to the far wall.

"Wh-where am I-I?" she stuttered, frantically looking around until her eyes landed on me.

"You!" she said, anger and fire lighting up her gray eyes.

"You fucking stalker. I'll get you for this!"

I raised my eyebrow. She was calling me the stalker? That was rich. She was the one that stowed away in my damn helicopter and broke the fucking thing.

"You certainly wake up more like a dragon than a princess." I mused.

She stared at me, confusion and anger melding into her eyes.

"What were you doing playing hide and seek in my aircraft?" I scolded, not giving a damn if she looked like a doe-eyed deer.

"What?" she said, looking around again. "Where am I?"

Sighing, I gestured around the stall, a few horses whining with annoyance that their sleep was disturbed.

"Home sweet bumfuck home," I sang, but she continued to glare at me.

I could see her carefully making a move to stand, and I braced myself, my stance ready to disarm her. I didn't know what she could do besides stab me in the eye with some hay, but knowing her, she was likely to try.

She charged at me with a growl. I was sure she thought she was ferocious. But before she could reach me, she slipped on one of the lovely cow pies in the field, and she fell right on her behind. Her head bounced off the ground with a thud, and she stilled.

Walking over to her, I tapped her with my boot. Her eyes flew open and stared right at me.

"Lucius?" she said in a daze.

I gave her my best smolder. "Yeah, Zaika, still me."

Zaika was the word for bunny in my native tongue, and the way she was bouncing around with her personality right now, the word bunny was damn accurate. She held her head, rubbing and wincing as she sat up.

"Wanna tell me why the fuck you sabotaged my helicopter?" She paled, her eyes darting to the door. "Uh, uh, uh, Little Shadow," I chastised, blocking her view. "You know the rules. When you try to kill a man, you owe him your presence at least."

She scoffed at me—the strange fear from before completely gone. Staring at her and shaking my head, I said, "You're a weird one, you know that?"

She stilled, her notorious glare flashing at me as I grinned at her.

"Where's your passenger?" she said, and my smile dropped. So, she knew my sister was with me and still tried to kill me.

"What passenger?" I lied, lazily leaning on the stall frame.

A horse's ass was getting dangerously close to my face, so I jumped off and walked closer to her.

"Get some sleep, Little Shadow," I said, yawning and plopping down beside her on the semi-soft, but mostly 'scratchy as fuck' hay.

She didn't hit me again. That was a plus. Her body heat and sweet, earthy scent cocooned me. She didn't wiggle away, and though we didn't spoon like in a rom-com, she did lay down and didn't move away from me.

I got lucky because she drifted off to sleep.

Sighing, I closed my eyes. Her scent and body were so close to my damn dick that it didn't know it was time to let me sleep. I turned my head, staring at her perfect body, her silky blonde hair, thick black lashes, puffy lips, and big tits.

My mouth watered. The memory of her honey taste was fresh and vivid in my mind.

I needed to taste her again.

I was robbed of getting to taste her straight from the source. The one night our bodies allowed that damn pull to happen, I hadn't been allowed the absolute pleasure of tasting her sweet pussy.

That was not fair.

The sleeping princess moaned as I ran my fingertips softly over her nipples. The blue fabric tightened in a spiral as they hardened.

Breathing a sigh of contentment at this princess's pure beauty, I carefully got up, not knowing if she'd wake as the princess or the dragon.

My cock throbbed in unison with my heart. "Beggars can't be choosers."

I nudged her thighs open, her black shorts giving me a peekaboo of her nice-shaven pussy. "Naughty girl, you're not wearing panties," I said with a moan, my cock throbbing in approval.

Pulling out my pocketknife from my boot, I flipped it open and sliced the offending shorts away. They fell apart on her creamy hourglass hips.

"Fuck." I groaned, the persistent appendage rubbing into the hay bale under her.

She moaned a sleepy, wistful sound.

"You want my mouth, my Little Shadow? Do you want me to make your sweet pussy weep?"

She continued to moan sleepy sighs as she shifted, opening herself to me even more.

I grabbed her hips, wrapping my arms under her. Taking handfuls of her thick delicious ass, I dove into her heat. The honey taste exploded in my mouth.

She was addictive.

A fucking drug.

My drug.

Moaning, I sucked on her more, lapping all of her juices and swirling my tongue on her clit. Her breathy moans switched to whimpers, and her closed eyes bounced as she rocked into my face.

"Mmm." She undulated her body, causing her core to roll onto my mouth. Deeper, harder, faster. I drew her orgasm out of her with heavy, languid licks and kisses to her sensitive little nub.

Nipping it lightly, I felt her gasp.

"Lucius..." she moaned, her whole body flooding my mouth with a sweet and slight hint of come.

I was soaked, and I was fucking overjoyed. I loved it when she coated me in her very own perfume. I'd wear her taste every day if I could.

Realizing she had said my name, even sleeping as she came was just as intoxicating as her taste, if not more. Standing up, I threw off the borrowed jeans. My whole body felt tight and painfully swollen. Kneeling and watching those eyelids dance, I opened her pretty little mouth and shoved myself home.

Chapter 23

Ember

I rode out the dream, floating on the cloud of pleasure with Lucius buried deep into my core. The orgasm was so powerful that it shook my very world. His skilled tongue and gorgeous body were just bonuses. Damn, he was dangerous. My very own poison. Ha. I guess this Snow White ate the poisoned apple.

My dream shifted. The beautiful water that was flowing around me, Lucius's tongue and lips crashing over me like the waves around us, morphed. Into something dark. No, not my dreams. My vision. The water…it was choking me, and I couldn't breathe. Scratching at my throat and trying to gasp for air, I panicked, not breathing… going…to die. White spots blew across my eyelids, and suddenly, I was awake.

Lucius and his thick cock were choking me. His thick-tatted hands held me down, and his face contorted in ecstasy. Pain and fire scratched at my throat, and he finally pulled free. Hot jets of come branded my face, my chest, and my mouth. Everywhere. He was everywhere.

Staring at him and unable to catch my breath, he smiled. Sweat dripped down his body, his shirt was soaked, his tan muscles rippling, and pieces of hay and dirt were stuck to him in random places.

"Well, I guess a kiss does wake up Snow White after all," he joked, laughing as I steadied my breathing. "On both lips."

I wanted to smack him. He just laughed again, stretching and yawning.

"Do you often fuck sleeping women?" I groused.

He shrugged. "We didn't fuck, sweetheart." He did a kissy face at me, and I threw a handful of hay at him.

"No, you'd be the first princess. Don't you feel honored?"

I rolled my eyes. "Lucky me."

He winked at me. "Oh, I know. You're welcome."

He yawned and walked back over to me, pushing my arms down. I wiggled, trying to free my hands, unsure what he was doing now.

He grumbled, "Sit still, woman. You're already a lumpy ass pillow so behave."

I was flabbergasted. This man, this insane man…no, this insane killer was using me as a fucking pillow?

I was unable to voice my shock because I was stunned at his audacity. Even more so when his soft snores drifted up to my ears minutes later.

Unbelievable.

Eyeing the exit, I raised my body.

His hand shot out and flicked me on the nose. "Now, now, Little Shadow. I am too fucking tired. Go to sleep. You can run from me tomorrow."

Blinking and rubbing my nose, feeling like a scolded puppy, I tried to push him off of me. But no matter how hard I pushed, he remained with his head on my lap and his arms firmly wrapped around my thighs.

"Fuck you, lard ass," I huffed, straining some more to get him off my leg.

He chuckled. His hot breath hit my clit, which made me jolt.

"Later, Little Shadow. Right now fucking eat an apple already and sleep."

Grumbling and knowing I was in no way getting up, I laid back and closed my eyes. The next thing I knew, I felt my eyes drifting shut.

I woke up and saw the big scary psycho sleeping soundly, curled up like a giant teddy bear on my thighs. He looked almost innocent when he slept.

Intrigued at this sleeping prince, I ran my fingertips over his strong jaw, his skin so soft and not at all matching the insane killer he was. He sighed in dreamy bliss, snuggling closer to me. I eyed my boot. Knowing damn well my dagger was in it.

I needed this infuriating man out of my way. He would forever stop me from getting to his sister, and I had to. She was the leader. The fucking queen. All this time I expected a man to be at the wheel, but I should have known the evil queen would be the ultimate contender.

Carefully, I reached into my boot, using my fingertips to feel for the handle.

Lucius stole my dagger and I was left with the stupid metal blade that didn't do much damage, but if I was quick enough I just needed one good slice.

Holding the knife above my head, poised over the sleeping prince beneath me, I hesitated...

Why did I hesitate?

Closing my eyes to center myself, I took a deep breath and began counting.

One...

Two...

I felt myself being slammed down onto the ground, my knife thrown away from my grip. Opening my eyes, I saw Lucius.

Surprised, angry, and something else...

"Well, if you wanted to play dirty, you only had to ask," he said, holding my wrists above my head and locking my pelvis down with his own.

Calculated mischief played on his features. Reaching down into his own boot, he pulled my dagger out from the sole. He twirled it in my face, taunting me.

"You want to play with knives?" His voice was raspy from sex and sleep. "Let's play."

Before I could protest, he took the dagger and sliced my shirt in two. The two sides fell apart, sliding down my sides. My breasts puckered up, teased by the cool air.

"You're so fucking beautiful," he said in awe.

The comment stunned me.

Besides, I wasn't going to struggle. It would only make him happier if I did. I needed to save my energy for later. Dipping his head down, he popped my nipple in his mouth, sucking and tantalizing the bud until I was curling my toes. Biting my bottom lip to keep from moaning, I swallowed hard. He laughed his musical laugh.

"Oh, sweet Little Shadow. Don't worry," he crooned, a dark promise in his gaze. "I'm going to make you scream."

Swallowing again and him biting so hard on my nub, I saw blood as it began to well onto my skin. His eyes transfixed onto those droplets.

"My family, as you probably know by now," he said conversationally, grabbing my wrists in one grip and twirling my dagger in his fingers with the other. "We are from the Russian gang known as Moya Kotva."

Leaning down, he licked my lip, the metallic taste of my very life on his tongue.

Going to my ear, the red liquid still on his lips, he whispered, "My. Blood."

I had a feeling that Lucius was part of something big, but I didn't realize how big it was until this very moment.

"Alyosha Puriya," I stated, my only knowledge of its leader.

Lucius looked into my eyes. Studying me and trying to figure out something just by looking into my eyes.

"My father always has been an exhibitionist. Loves everyone knowing his name." Lucius's face darkened. "He's who you've been looking for, Snow White. Not my sister. You kill her, and you've killed an innocent woman who just happens to have the wrong lineage."

I pondered that. Alyosha was big news. He controlled all of Russia and half the states.

"You were sent here to find me." I put together why a don's son would be shipped off to America. Certainly not just to be a playboy. "*Black Mirrors* is a front for most, if not all, of the dirty money."

I continued watching Lucius. He didn't deny it. He just let me put each puzzle piece together.

"Eilizaveta is your twin sister, and she was brought here too because you wouldn't kill me?"

Lucius scoffed. "No, Little Shadow, that's where you're wrong. My sister was kidnapped in Russia in her own home. She was supposed to supersede our father, but my cousin had other plans."

Hatred radiated off him. His grip on my wrists became bruising.

"Markus," I said aloud.

"I shouldn't be surprised you've been my shadow." Lucius was grinning now.

"Only returning the favor." I smiled back, sickly sweet.

"Where did you get this dagger?" he said, twisting the intricate handle and looking at the beauty of it.

"My father made it." I tried not to show my pain, but it was too evident.

"I am sorry," he said, making me blink in surprise. "What? I do have a soul. It's just painted black."

I snorted. "Yeah, and mine's red."

He eyed my chest, the exposed feeling making me shiver. "I love you in red."

With that he ran my blade over my chest, a slight red line painting me. I gasped at the feeling of pain and pleasure. That secret euphoric sting made me feel so alive. Lucius noticed my reaction. My body practically levitated under him.

"Interesting," he chuckled, taking that sharp tip across my belly, the cut a bit deeper, and the blood dripping down my side.

"My Little Shadow likes to bleed for me."

I whimpered, not caring that he was teasing me. I just wanted this. No, I needed it when so much pain was carried inside me all the time. It felt so freeing to let some of it out. My pelvis ground into his hardening crotch, and his moans made my body shake.

"Careful." He groaned, meeting my thrusts, gripping my wrists even tighter.

He liked this, too. "I can take your life so easily. Watch you drain drip by drip."

I tightened my jaw. "But you won't, Lucius," I said, knowing it was true, just like I knew my hand would never end his life either.

"We're connected. Someway. Somehow. You're infuriating and annoying, and most of the time, I want to kill you. But I can't. You're my true equal. My own fucking poison."

Lucius's jaw tightened, his eyes growing heated and heavy.

"Ever since I followed you, Little Shadow, I've been hooked. Unhinged. I wanted to kill you for so long, kept trying to figure out how you're so fucking smart. You always evaded me at every turn. Drove me absolutely mad. I have never hunted someone down for so long without making the killing strike, but then I realized…"

Those melting emerald green eyes bore into me. With a roar of abandon, he released my wrists, grabbed my face, and smashed his lips onto mine.

With a soft whisper on my lips, he said, "You. Are. Mine."

Chapter 24

My Little Shadow had promised to leave. Her heated sex and pouty red lips were so fresh on my tongue.

I felt drunk as I dragged my ass into the little cottage. Gertrude already had fresh bacon sizzling on the stove despite it being only five am or so. I didn't see the head of the house but assumed maybe he went off to tend to his livestock. They had, after all, gotten the scare of their plump ass lives.

My sister sat primly with her hands steepled. The effort she was trying to put forth was astounding. Her critical lessons in etiquette and manners were not at all beaten out of her.

I supposed those hours with a band tied to your chest, crucifying you to a chair, were not easily forgotten. Maybe Markus didn't have worse torture to dish out than our dear old daddy.

"You've been out late," my twin noted, staring at my disheveled appearance and swollen lips.

"Find a pig to frolic with, brother?"

I scowled at her, the thought of kissing livestock disgusting.

"How did you sleep, sestra?" I said, ignoring her greeting altogether, plopping down, and quickly swallowing the glass of freshly squeezed orange juice.

"Like the dead."

It was a bit morbid for her life, but she always had a flair for the dramatics.

"Funny. So, we're going to the location in a few hours. I walked to a gas station and used the phone booth. Did you know they still had those damn things? Anyway, I talked to Reggie. He said they would come pick us up here. There's a private airstrip near here that they'd paid off."

Eili, well Ivy, nodded curtly, standing up and brushing her tight black pantsuit down and smoothing her white blouse.

"Good. I'm going to go home. You can go take care of things without me."

Nothing like sister Teresa to make me do her dirty work. I could tell she felt conflicted. Killing this girl wasn't fun. It was business. Markus said she was a cop's sister. If we let her go, she'd tell her sister everything, and orange wasn't my color.

"Riiiight."

I looked at Gertrude slaving over the stove, making scrambled eggs. Flashbacks of my mother's dark curly hair hunched over the stove, making blini, syrniki, and kasha for my sister and I flooded my mind. It was such a small piece of happiness in my life—such simplistic times.

Looking at my sister, I wished that kind of peace for her. I wished her mother could come back to care for her, to offer the comfort she surely needed. She was always so strong, but even warriors needed protection.

"I love you, sestra," I mumbled awkwardly at the door frame.

Eili, fuck…Ivy looked back at me. Her amber eyes pooled with tears. "I love you, brâtva."

Boston was busy and loud, and the seagulls sounded like they were barking. The accents made my ears bleed, and I honestly couldn't figure out why the fuck Markus would hide some woman away here.

Ivy said he had a liking for this girl. That he'd gotten attached, and in his sick world, not torturing her was being a king.

I stared at the note, my sister's neat print on the paper. A logo of the hotel, she had copied down with the bloody scrawl marks that Markus had originally made.

I stopped at the crosswalk light, walking in the blazing heat because these fucking weirdos never used cars, apparently.

Feeling like Thomas, the fucking, Train, bustling along with these ignorant phone-addicted city slickers, I turned a corner and stopped to look up at the huge ass skyscraper.

"Is this the Inn on Brookline Drive?" I said to a lady passing by and pointed up at the hulking hotel.

The lady squinted, looking up at the building with me. "Yeah, doll. Just in that car park!"

She didn't have an inside voice at all. I cringed, waiting for my eardrums to readjust.

"The caw part?" I said, confused. Seriously, what is with this accent?

"Straight to the center, go in the tunnel, press number two, and boom…the receptionist will be there, sweetheart!"

I didn't catch much, but something about taking a shit. Nodding anyway and fearful for my hearing, I crossed the street to the car park, seeing a tunnel that led to a swanky elevator.

Smiling at the camera as usual, I checked my suit and tie.

Making my way to the receptionist, I plastered on my dirtiest smile, showing some of my manly chest hair.

The receptionist, however, was not a hot blonde, a sexy Asian, or even a bodacious ass black woman. No…what I got was a fucking man. Not only a man but one who looked like he could eat me.

I lost the smile and walked to the desk. "Excuse me, sir. I'm Detective John Waters, and there's an investigation in room seven eighty-three. I need to investigate immediately."

The gruff guy gave me a once over, not looking at all impressed.

"You got a badge, pig?"

Cursing myself and seeing my shit-eating grin on multiple cameras, I sighed. "Yeah, I think I left it in my squad car."

Putting my tail between my legs, I walked out of the fucking office.

Maybe I can scale the building like Spider-Man.

Walking back toward the elevator, I caught a glimpse of a pale blonde's hair near some pointless plant by the door.

My eyes narrowing, I walked over to it, casually leaning on the frame.

She didn't bother hiding. No, instead, she tumbled out, laughing her tight little ass off.

"I'm not amused," I said, watching her giggle, completely unfazed. It would be kind of cute if it weren't directed at me.

"Real smooth, Casanova," she said, her snorts still laced with laughter.

"Meh. He's not really my type."

She laughed again, her eyes twinkling with genuine joy. I liked seeing her happy. It made me feel...warm.

"Guess you can do better, Little Shadow?" I taunted.

She smirked at me, her eyes devious. Standing up and shaking that sexy ass to the counter, she threw me a wink over her shoulder.

Sure enough, within a minute of stuttering from the idiot male and flirtatious giggling from Ember, she was waltzing back with a shiny metallic card key in her hand. I raised my eyebrow, eating my humble pie with dignity. She giggled again, raising up on her top toes and kissing me on the cheek. My cheek flamed red hot with her brand, and I felt myself blushing.

Godamnit…this woman's fire would surely melt me.

Chapter 25

Ember

After gloating and dancing around Lucius for a few minutes on the seventh-floor hallway, taunting him with my prize, I finally gave him the keycard and stepped back, prepared for anything. I didn't actually know why the fuck he was here. He said he was looking for something, but what? Jewels? Money?

Lucius placed his ear to the door and held up his finger to hold still as he listened.

Either not hearing anything or threatening, he opened the door. The inside area of the suite was big. The place was decked out like it was a playroom for millionaires who came here to pay for private hookers they hid from their wives. The screen door led to a balcony with a beautiful view. The screen door was wide open, letting fresh, beautiful air inside. The wallpaper was a boring gray wash, with a small kitchenette to the side and a big jacuzzi tub in the center.

Nothing really struck me as off until I saw small red marks on the floor.

Blood.

So this wasn't about retrieving money, then.

Lucius was searching. He began opening doors and closets, but there was nothing in the few small rooms he searched. His eyes became fixated on the handle of a door that was closed at the end of the hallway.

Opening it up, I hid behind him, not knowing if I really wanted to see whatever was in there. Lucius shielded me. His muscular body stepped right in front. I could hear whimpering—the sounds of a woman gagged, actually.

He had a hostage?

As crazy as Lucius was, I didn't take him for fucking with innocents. But this girl didn't seem like a bad guy. She seemed caught in a war she didn't even know existed. I peeked through his arms and saw a brown-haired girl, a bit beaten up, but mostly just some bruises on her neck and thighs. She was in shorts that had little red stains on them.

Her shirt was torn up, and her chest was exposed. There were gashes on her stomach. This Markus guy was fucked up.

At least Lucius was here to free her…wasn't he?…

Getting a sinking feeling in my gut, I realized he wasn't wearing a mask, a hoodie, a black coat. Nothing. His beautiful face was on full display.

He wasn't here to save this girl.

He was here to kill her.

Well fuck that.

"Hey!" I snapped, Lucius spinning around to face me, surprise on his features.

The girl was screaming now in the back—the gag muffled her cries for help.

"I don't kill anyone who doesn't deserve it," I said, my eyes narrowing on him and his gun jutting out of his pants pocket. The little nozzle on the top must be the silencer.

He frowned, shaking his head. "I don't like it, Little Shadow, but it's gotta be done. She knows too much."

I vehemently shook my head. "No."

Lucius sighed. "Look, if you don't want to be here, go back to the lobby. I'll meet you when it's over."

The girl's cries became louder. The sound of a wooden chair cracking onto the floor, and she bounced.

"You don't want to cross this line, Lucius. Once you do, you'll never be the same. You're not like your cousin. Let her go."

Lucius held the gun, his hands hesitant on the handle.

"I don't have a choice," he said, pulling it out and aiming it toward the prisoner.

I smashed into him, taking him to the ground. The girl bounced up and down on the chair but stopped when she saw me grappling for the gun with Lucius.

Her eyes looked haunted and confused.

Lucius spun me around again, and I locked onto her eyes one more time. Did she look elated? I backflipped out of his way, turning to her. No, she carried a look of defeat.

Fighting with Lucius hand to hand was like smashing my fists into fucking solid walls. I could tell he wasn't trying to hurt me but subdue me and that pissed me off more. I wasn't some meek weakling.

Throwing harder punches and getting more kicks in, I saw the girl struggling with the tie around her hands. Her raw wrists wriggled, and she finally freed herself. Instead of doing the sane thing of leaving and saving her skin, she jumped on top of Lucius and started throwing her own punches and kicks.

The gun was thrown outside the door, sliding along the floor to the damn balcony, and all our tangled limbs managed to sprawl into the living room area.

I broke free of the battle. Our strength and wits were too evenly matched. With neither of us winning or losing, I saw the girl run to the gun, her bravery and strength astounding. Running out to the balcony with shaking hands, she picked up the Berretta and pointed it straight at Lucius.

My heartbeat was beating in my chest, my world moving in slow motion. Lucius was too focused on not hurting me and wasn't paying attention to the armed woman on the balcony. I grabbed my dagger from my boot, watching in disbelief as it flew through the air into the heart of the woman.

Her blue-grey eyes stared down at the knife, the blood trickling down the front of her body as her gaze settled on mine. Confusion, pain, and betrayal were written in those beautiful eyes as the gun fell to the ground. The woman dropped from the balcony, taking my last shred of humanity with her soul.

Chapter 26

Ella

I held the phone to my ear, the voices fading away as they said the words, I'd been waiting to hear for nearly a month were spoken. "They found Cassie."

It was like a dream—my body was floating and not hearing another damn word, and my happiness was the only thing keeping me grounded enough to focus. I knew Quinn was trying to talk to me, but I was on autopilot. My mind's only thought was me getting to my sister.

We rode in a plane. The hours ticked by fast, too fast. Nothing was going to stop me from seeing her and holding her. I was never letting her go again.

We arrived at a big ass hotel.

Not sure why she'd be here. But hey, I wasn't complaining. Going off the grid was fine. I would allow anything now that I knew she was here.

Chief Doger himself, the fucking snake, was here. Strange, but I appreciated the welcome wagon.

Cassie deserved it.

I loved her so much. She deserved everything.

I kept thinking about what TV shows I could finally binge that she'd bugged me for years about, all the weird foods she wanted to try from different places in the world, and how she begged me to paint my nails. She always said she wanted to make me look like a girl for once.

I smiled, looking at my nails and imagining what god-awful color she was going to put on me.

Whatever. If it was bubblegum pink, I'd rock it for her. For Cassie. My sister.

Quinn wrapped his arms around me. The big man always gave bear hugs. He was such a nice guy.

"Ella," he said, his voice cold, hesitant.

That was strange. Why would he be all moody now?

I was about to see my sister.

"Your sister is in there," Chief Doger said. Not a care in the world for that guy, but I didn't give a shit. Cassie was here.

Slipping free of Quinn's arms, I ignored him, running for the door. My sister's embrace waited for me on the other side.

"Cassie! I'm here—"

My heart stilled.

Stopping dead in my tracks, I looked around. There were people dressed in white scrub outfits, a yellow band slashing across the door frame. The air chilled around me, and a clear tarp on the ground covered a river of crimson underneath it.

Did Cassie kill someone? That wasn't like her, but maybe it was necessary. She always was a fighter. I was proud of her. Walking forward, I spotted Ally with usual morgue get-up on, and her face saddened for the dead person my sister was forced to kill.

"Ella," she said, her eyes swollen in red-rimmed tears.

"I'm so sorry." I shrugged. "Honestly, I hope it doesn't hurt her too badly, but a girl's got to do what a girl's got to do, right? She's not in trouble, is she? It was clearly self-defense." A knife was placed on a steel cart, red blood coating the crime scene bag it was placed in. Was Cassie going to be in legal trouble? Ah, hell, I would get her the best lawyer.

Quinn caught up to me, he and Ally exchanging a look.

"Guys, it's okay! Cassie had to do it. It wasn't her fault."

Quinn swallowed and lightly squeezed my shoulder. It was cute that they loved me and were worried so much about my sister, a murderer. But I would help her get out of this legal shit.

"Ella," Quinn said, grabbing my shoulders gently but firmly.

I furrowed my brows.

"Micah, please. I know she's in trouble, but please let me see her. I need to find out what happened so I can help her get a lawyer."

Now Quinn furrowed his brows, looking to Ally and back to me. I didn't like this. Why were they keeping me from Cassie?

"Ella…" Quinn said again, holding my hand and leading me to the plastic tarp. "Cassie isn't in trouble. She didn't kill anyone," he said carefully.

Snapping on gloves, I grabbed the edge of the tarp.

"I'm so sorry, Ella," Ally murmured again.

Wait, no. That didn't make any sense. Cassie had to have killed someone. She had to be in trouble. She had to, or that would mean she—

Quinn carefully pulled the tarp up.

My beautiful sister Cassandra Marie Fox was lying in a pool of blood, her eyes open, her face full of betrayal and pain, and my world shattered.

Chapter 27

Ember

I was a murderer.

I had taken many lives, but never one that didn't deserve it. That girl would forever haunt me. Haunt my dreams. Her eyes were so trusting, and she was trying to help me, for god's sake.

And I killed her…ended her life…for Lucius.

The man stirred beside me. His sighs and snores filled the club. I'd sold my soul to the devil. Eili, his sister, wasn't going to die at my hand. But someone was going to feel the pain of the life lost. Someone was going to regret the day they were born.

"What are you plotting, Little Shadow?" Lucius said. His yawn was a grumble as he rested his hands behind his head, looking over at me.

"I'm going to kill your father," I stated.

I didn't expect Lucius to laugh, but there he was, laughing his ass off and rumbling the big king-size bed we were lying on.

"Fine, sure thing, Little Shadow." He smoothed my hair. "But first, you may want to kill his partner."

I furrowed my eyebrows, annoyed that he was making me wait.

"The big daddy chief of police is the supplier for good-old Rochy Roch."

I blinked.

Of course, law enforcement would have some dirty pigs, but I have to say I wasn't expecting the head of the entire department to be using his little soldiers to distribute drugs.

"That's unexpected," I said, and Lucius laughed.

"Nah, all pigs roll in shit. It makes sense they'd take any scrap given to them."

I rolled my shoulders, sitting up and rubbing my sore neck. My fucking face even hurt.

"You expect me to infiltrate the police?" I said as incredulity flooded through my body.

Lucius shrugged, a huge yawn and stretch accompanied by his rumble of silent chuckling.

"I mean, you could always just steal one of his little piggies."

I pondered that. Better idea, I could lay in bed, and he could go and get a toy soldier.

"Actually, that's your job. You owe me. Ya know, for stealing my innocence and all...you're unobservant. I saved your ungrateful ass."

The devil didn't like being called weak. I grinned.

"Ha. If you want to kill the king, go after his guardsman yourself."

I pouted, jutting out my lip. I knew he loved to bite.

"I could," I said, letting the covers fall to my waist. Now, my breasts were exposed, and his eyes zeroed in on my nipples.

Swinging my legs from the bed, I sashayed to the bathroom. Feeling his eyes burn into my ass the whole walk there. Turning on the spray of the warm water, I chuckled, hearing the thunderous booming of his usually quiet footsteps.

"Excuse you, woman," he said, watching me from the glass.

I shrugged, sudsing my hair with sweet-smelling shampoo.

"Excuse yourself," I said. Catching his reflection in the glass, I tried to hide my laughter.

He was fuming. Stepping into the wall in the shower, he looked behind me, his shadow engulfing mine in front of me.

"Little Shadow," he warned, his soaked shirt flesh against my back.

Why did he never take off his shirt? I wondered.

Oh well, another time.

"Yes?" I said innocently, running my soapy hands down my body, making sure to linger on my clit and ass. His breath caught.

"You are the most addictive poison I've ever had. I didn't take a bite of the apple. I fucking swallowed it whole."

Now, I was laughing out loud. Turning to him to see his defeat, but as soon as I did he grabbed me by the throat, slammed me into the shower wall, his knee coming up between my thighs.

I gasped at the friction, the pleasure and pain building like an inferno in my stomach. He was grinning now. His smirk was triumphant as he whispered in my ear while sliding his dick along my slick core.

"Remember, next time you use a pawn to corner the king's knight," he purred.

"That someone may just take advantage of the queen."

That was the first time he hadn't called me Little Shadow, but he referred to me as the well and true leader.

"Yeah?" I moaned, my voice barely audible as he squeezed tighter around my throat.

"Yes, baby. Fuuuck, yes."

He took a fistful of my hair, flipped me over, and pressed my chest into the cold stone tile lining the back wall. I felt him yank off his sopping-wet shirt and toss it with a thump onto the floor. I tried to turn, tried to look at his delicious body, but he tightened his grip on my hair, his strange symbol tattoos rippling. My head was jerked up, the pull on my hair demanding and in control.

"Naughty girl." He slapped my ass, leaving a blazing red handprint on my left cheek.

I hissed, the sting of the slap mixing with the heat of the spray.

"You know what happens to nosy little asses, Kotinyick?" I whimpered, his fingers sliding inside my wet pussy. Quickly, he gave me a punishing smack to the lips.

"I said…" he repeated, scraping his teeth along my jaw, biting my neck like a fucking vampire. A deep engraved mark. A brand. "Do you know…"

"What happens."

Smack.

"To nosy."

Rub.

"Little."

Smack.

"Asses."

He took a handful of my ass and bit down hard. Whimpering and wanting my pleasure so badly, I pushed my ass on him, grinding my hips.

"N-no," I said.

He slipped his two long, thick, talented fingers inside me.

He fucked me hard, unabandoned, and faster than my eyes could track. My screams echoed off the shower walls, creating a hum around us. My orgasm was so powerful that it absolutely took me to my knees. The sweet liquid spilled from me like a dam bursting. My head was still angled up, but I felt him smile on the skin of my back.

"That's right," he said, popping his fingers in my mouth. "Good fucking girl. My good fucking girl. Now…Taste your come. Remember what only I can do to you," he demanded, gagging me with his slippery digits.

He let go of my hair, smoothing it down my back and leaving trails of light kisses on my neck, tracing the faint lines of his fingertips.

"Now," he said, allowing me to turn around and marvel at his glorious muscled chest and abs. "Answer my question, my queen."

My brain was completely addled with sex as I tried to remember the question, but his cock was thick and in command, jutting out from his hips. The veins on the top bulge, pulsating, making it bounce. He watched my gaze, moaning at my praise.

"Fuck, Little Shadow," he said in a hoarse whisper.

"If you keep looking at my cock like that," he warned, stepping closer, pushing that thick rod into my stomach. "I'm going to make you choke on it."

The promise was dangerous, sensual, and true.

"Good." I breathed, challenging him with a look as I leaned down on my knees—the bite of the tile floor I ignored with him so close to my parting lips. Lucius groaned, my breath hot on his balls, the sound of a beast fighting for control.

He was gripping a shower bar, his knuckles white with strain as he allowed me to have this control. I slipped my tongue along his head, feeling the silky-smooth texture pop in my mouth, my lips closing around the head and teasing his slit with my tongue.

"Your forms of torture are very cruel," he grunted, sweat beading on his skin.

I laughed around his member, the vibration making him stand straight up. I took my free hand and gently kneaded his testicles, rolling my knuckles into his asshole. His eyes closed, and I wanted to take a picture of his absolute beauty at this moment.

Wrapping my other hand around his base, I twisted my wrist slightly, going up and down, using my mouth to follow my hand.

He moaned in approval, his grip so tight on the tile rack that I could hear little cracks occurring.

Going faster, I tested his massive length, wondering if I could even take him fully.

Not giving me an option, his control breaking like that tile, he slammed my head onto his cock. The thick length filled my mouth, gagging me, thrusting to the back of where my throat allowed.

It felt like he was bending down my throat, his impossibly long, thick cock throbbing in my mouth. Tears streamed down my face, and my ability to breathe was completely gone. He gave me short breaks as he pulled my head off just enough to gasp for air and slammed me back down to nearly his base.

"You look so pretty when you cry."

I looked into his eyes. The water, tears, and saliva coated my face, dripping down my chest and sliding to my heated pussy. He moaned, picking up my body and spinning me around upside down. My mouth never left his thickness. It simply did a corkscrew.

My gasp was silenced by his thrusts as he dove his mouth onto my cunt. The feeling was so heady that I nearly came right then. The rush of blood to my head and lack of oxygen had me dizzy. Lucius had turned me away from the water, his hair dripping water down onto my throbbing pussy. His fucking tongue was magic. It felt like he hadn't been sucking my clit and lapping my juices for more than a minute before I felt myself coming so hard my eyes saw black spots.

Having no time to catch my breath, Lucius bucked, his own cry echoing in my ears, and he shot hot jets of come down my throat. I felt complete at that moment. An unexplainable feeling of right... and maybe something else. Lucius flipped me back over, sudsing up his hands and gently washing my body. He placed a light kiss on the top of my hair.

Staring into my eyes, he whispered. "You are mine, Little Shadow. Do with me what you will because I, too, belong to you."

Chapter 28

Lucius

Goddamn, did I feel pussy whipped right now.

Stalking a fucking Thor-looking cop and his partner all because my Little Shadow told me to do it.

Shaking my head, I ran my hand down my face. The power of pussy, I mused to myself.

Watching the two people walk into a bar, I noticed their pig uniforms and faces glowing with egotistical self-righteous bullshit.

Realizing the male blond cop was the one who was following my sister around like a guard dog made this all the more fun—two birds kind of deal.

I didn't know who the fuck the girl was with him, but I didn't really care.

Stalking behind the bar, I made my way to the alley. Seeing a stray dog, I threw an old granola bar his way and slumped down in the alley. My truck was parked right by the door. A convenient little parking spot to, say, abduct some dirty cops?

Taking out my gun, I shot a round into a hole in the tin barrel a few yards away. Dead fish were swimming in their afterlife, pouring from the holes. The pretty boy cop, right on cue, stormed outside the bar, making a beeline for the stinky fountain I created for him.

The girl was trailing behind him, perfect.

Two knights down.

Checkmate, baby.

Walking into the shadows, I decided to take out the female first. I never underestimated these women. They were strong little fuckers, crafty and agile on their feet. Smashing my gun in the back of her head, she went down. I winced at the volume, realizing that it was a bit of a hard hit. Blood welled at the wound, and I cursed.

The male cop noticed me instantly and started grappling with me. I had to give him some credit. For a cop, he was strong, and he definitely fought dirty. Kicking near my balls and twisting his fingers into my pressure points, I enjoyed this challenge.

But I couldn't fuck around too long. My sleeping queen awaited for her prize.

Slipping my gun from my pocket, I didn't hold it aimed at him. No, I aimed it at the cop on the ground. The big man stilled. His holy justice act may be for real, or maybe he had a loyalty to this girl. Who knew?

"As fun as tussling with you is, pretty boy, Imma need you to get your ass in the trunk. Play nice, and I'll let the pretty girl live."

I didn't think that was entirely true, and I wasn't sure she was alive, to be honest. I really did do a number on her head, and her hair was matted with blood.

He held up his hands and said, "All right. Just don't hurt her."

We both were probably thinking the same thing, but the hope was prominent in his voice.

Shrugging and flipping the girl over my shoulder, I gently plopped her in my trunk, guiding the male with my gun in behind her.

"My truck has been revamped not to have an emergency latch

or the ability to kick out one of my precious taillights," I warned. "So be nice to her, yeah?"

The guy tightened his jaw, but like a good little boy, he cradled the girl's bleeding head and laid down.

Getting back to the club, I looked around for my Little Shadow and realized she wasn't around. Maybe she went to get some dinner or something. Whatever, that girl was always running off somewhere.

Opening the trunk, I gave the male detective some duct tape and a metal set of cuffs.

"These bracelets will look lovely on you," I said, smirking as he clicked the fuzzy pink handcuffs on his wrists. Tightening it myself, I grabbed the tape and smacked it on his lips.

Frowning at the girl, I realized she wasn't waking up. Damnit. Ember was going to be mad that I killed another "Innocent."

The pretty boy cop looked over at his partner and realized the same thing. Sadness and anger swirled in his blue eyes.

"Now, now, I won't have any of that big boy." I chastised. "You're a gift, and you need to play nice."

Those baby blues bore into me, daggers laced within his irises. His partner's blood was staining my damn trunk, and blood was a bitch to get out of upholstery. I decided he didn't need to look at his dead partner anymore and slipped one of my nice ties around his eyes.

I was generous like that.

Ember arrived a short while later. Waltzing up to me with Starbucks and a bagel in her hands. I grinned, kissing her deeply and giddy with my present locked in the other room for her. I decided it was best not to tell her about my accidental murder and just toss that lady in one of my expensive-ass rugs.

Her death cost me fifty grand. She went out in style. Reggie and Quiet an had taken her somewhere to dump her body in a grave, and I was saving the environment by letting her share someone else's.

"So what's this surprise you've been gloating about?" she said, her excitement evident even though she was trying to play it cool.

"Ya know," I shrugged. "Just the king's very own knight, baby."

Now, my queen audibly squealed. The sound was deafening and surprised me, considering she was no taller than my pec muscles. She bounced on her toes. Spinning around and continuing that awful "Eeee" noise.

I caught myself smiling. Unable to figure out the puzzle that was my Little Shadow.

My Shadow's eyes looked inquisitive as she stared at her prisoner. Not at all the way I've seen her with the drug dealers—my father's men.

"He's one of them," I told her, my gentle squeeze on her arm, assuring her I wasn't leaving.

"I don't know. He's too pretty to be dirty," she teased.

My jaw ticked, and she laughed, the man looking in her direction but not able to see her beauty.

Ha, motherfucker, I thought as I gazed at her beauty. The guy tilted his head, trying to hear or see her maybe. I threw a punch to his ear, smashing him to the ground. The chair went flying down with him. With a grunt, he blinked up at me. His dizzying gaze snapped to my girl's before closing. Ember looked at me with annoyance.

"Great job, Meathead," she chastised. Her hands on her hips.

"Now, he's unconscious, and we can't get any information out of him."

I shrugged. "He shouldn't have looked at what's mine."

Rolling her eyes, she looked down at the guy, my fire of jealousy licking up my neck like venom.

"Maybe we could keep him. He's cute."

That was it.

Smacking her ass hard, I threw her over my shoulder, walking to the bedroom to show her, for the next several hours, why she would never stare at another man again.

"I fucking own you, Lév," I said, tossing her down on the mattress and flipping her over. "Mind, soul, and body," I continued, ripping her pretty dress with my bare hands.

She gasped. The sting I laid on her ass was hard and sure.

"And for daring to look at another, man," I warned, cooling the burn with my tongue. "I'm going to make you scream my name. Only mine. Over and over and over."

Chapter 29

Ella

I woke up.

My head throbbed with a pulsing that felt like ice was embedded into my head. It had been this way for a while now, and the puffy eyes and swollen face were a constant these days. Yawning, the sleeping pills were making me laggy. I swung my feet out of my bed and blindly stumbled in the dark to my bathroom.

Trying to watch my step so I didn't step on Shadow or Mitzi, I walked the line about ten shuffles from the bed. But when I got there, instead of walking into my baby powder blue bathroom, I smashed straight into a wall. The thud knocked me on my ass.

I rubbed my head, staring in the dark at the solid block of plaster.

What the hell?

Getting into a crawl, I put my hands on the wall and followed it down the line. My confusion was building while my fingertips slid over the cool texture. Stopping abruptly at what felt like a wooden door, my panic rose.

I was not in my apartment.

Staying on the floor, I opened the door and pushed it open. Letting my eyes adjust to the moonlit space. There was a baby grand piano in the dark corner. There were blacked-out windows where I could only stare back at my reflection. There was even a bar with popcorn kernels in two separate bowls and some chocolate syrup next to some handcuffs.

What the fuck? Was I dreaming?

How had I landed myself in some funhouse mirror of kinky rich people?

Shaking my head, I walked along the tile, the cool texture leaving more goosebumps on my skin. I tried to make my footfalls silent, afraid of whoever may be here. After searching some of the closets and a big bathroom, I arrived at a staircase. The floor below me looked ominous and really dark.

Steeling myself, I took a deep breath and walked down the fancy staircase. Not having the best track record with staircases, I was wary of my last trip and hugged the corner of the railing. At the bottom floor, I nearly screamed. In the dim moonlight, it really was a funhouse of horrors. Mirrors lined the walls, a huge space with a disco ball at its center.

Trying not to walk into my own reflections that were fearfully staring back at me, I made my way around the mirrors to another bar. This one looked industrial. Million-dollar liquor, whiskeys, and wines gleamed with the light from the far window. At least these weren't completely blacked out. I could see the street outside, lit up by a streetlamp and a few car headlights.

Where the fuck was I?

Not ever having been here, I had no idea how or why I'd ended up here. Did I sleepwalk again? Breaking and entering while I was at it? I walked to the exit, a huge neon side indicating my escape, but I heard a thumping sound before I opened the door to leave.

Curiosity getting the best of me, I walked toward another door. This one was white and looked way less expensive than the theme of the other crap in here. Grumbling, I looked to see a strange contraption acting as a lock on it.

"Damnit." I looked around and tried to find something to disable this thing.

It had a fingerprint scanner and looked like something out of a spy movie.

Grabbing a bottle of whiskey that was probably ten times more than my apartment, car, and paycheck, I dumped it on the green lock. A sizzling and the green light flickered until making one last zapping noise before turning to black and falling to the floor with a thud.

The sound was loud, making it sound like a gunshot in the otherwise quiet room. There was a hum of the usual appliances, but I'd take that over that constant tick-tock sound at my place.

Opening the door, I wondered if I was about to star in those cheesy horror flicks with me being the moron who got eaten by a boogeyman, all because they'd checked out the noise and didn't just leave.

The thudding was louder now, and another sound...muffled yelling? Goosebumps pricked at my skin, uncertain about what I was about to find. At the bottom of the stairs, I couldn't see anything. I literally descended into darkness. It was even darker than the room I had awakened in.

Using my hands to guide me, and my ears to follow the thumping, I arrived at a door. This one was not locked with Inspector Gadget gizmos, thankfully. The thumping and muffled voice was so loud here that I could practically feel their body heat from the other side of the door. Opening the door, I stood still, my fear of the boogeyman stopping me in my tracks.

"H-Hello?" I said.

The thumping and muffled voice stopped.

"I'm here to help you," I said, trying to navigate myself in this pitch-black room.

I didn't know the condition of the prisoner, but the voice was deep, so I assumed it was a male. I could be saving a criminal who got in another criminal's way, but I couldn't surely leave this man here to be killed by the kinky rich people.

Catching the familiar scent of blood, I reached my hand out. Making contact with a big body, I ran my hand down, trying to locate whatever held the man prisoner.

Got it!

Smiling to myself, I undid the bindings and got hit with a fist so big I thought my jaw might have cracked. Screaming, I held my hands up to my face. The man mounted me, laying blows on my arms and sides.

I just saved a fucking hulk-of-a man, and my thanks would be death by a smashed facial bone.

"Stop!" I yelled, scooting backward, giving up on protecting anything but my major organs. "Please!"

A trance had taken over this guy. Pure survival kicked in, and he wasn't hearing a word. Out of the corner of my eye, I thought I saw an angel. Someone with black wavy hair and a handsome face descended the stairs, but pure, undiluted rage and worry were on his beautiful face.

Suddenly, the pain stopped.

The angel collided with the devil, allowing me to scramble up the stairs.

My ribs were broken. My face was at an all-time new swollen, and each step had me crying out in pain. Making it to safety, I hid behind the bar. My body was unable to really do more than that. The sounds of fighting and grunts continued. The fight brought itself up the stairs and right across the bar.

Steeling myself, I peered around the bar.

My heart absolutely stopped.

Quinn.

Micah Quinn was the prisoner. The man who beat me to a pulp and my angel?

The shady club owner, Lucius Vasiliev, was throwing punches, both men going hard and for the kill. They were evenly matched, however, and the fighting continued with the brutal expert brawl.

Godamnit...

Looking around for a weapon, I settled on a damn liquor bottle. Sneaking up as best as my whimpering ass could manage, neither male paying any attention to me, I waited for the perfect moment and brought the bottle down hard.

My victim crashed to the floor. Standing above him, I felt a strange sense of sadness mingled with guilt. My heart screaming at me to stop. He saved me from a beating, so what? That doesn't make him a prince. Right?

Quinn wouldn't have hurt me if he knew it was me.

The male was in rough shape from their fight, my blow to the head being the final straw that brought him down. He looked up at me. Confusion and pain lacing his angry features, and something else...sadness?

No.

His green eyes were gleaming with a look I knew all too well...betrayal.

Chapter 30

Lucius

G uard dog could hit. I'd give him that. My body was screaming at me. He was the best challenger I had fought in a while, but I couldn't enjoy it.

Ember was in danger. I had to protect my woman.

My body came to a stifling halt when my head felt like an anvil had dropped on me. Dizziness settling in, I couldn't hold myself up, the crash of the ground barely registering as I stared around in a blur.

Did the puppy get me? How?

I had been throwing the same amount of punches and jabs as he had. Maybe I slipped up, and he finally made a move.

One that was going to cost me.

My vision was starting 'the twinkle, twinkle, little stars' bit, and my head was throbbing. The blackness gripped me like a meat hook in my head. The last thing I saw before the darkness took me under was those haunting blue-gunmetal gray eyes staring down back into mine.

"Lucius Vasiliev." Detective Micah Morgan Quinn said to me. The shiner and busted lip I gave him shone in the painfully bright fluorescent light. "You are under arrest for the kidnapping and assault of me, Detective Quinn, from the Rochester Police Department."

He droned on and on about my rights.

"You're also being charged with the kidnapping, assault, and murder of Detective Emily Kinds."

I yawned.

"I don't recall killing anyone," I said, shrugging and leaning back in the chair as far as the handcuffs would allow.

I was going to get out of this.

I had to get back to Ember.

I had to make sure she was safe.

Did the police have her, too? She couldn't be linked to my crimes. She was smart. She had to have gotten out. The detective's jaw clenched, his good boy mask slipping, letting me see the murder in his eyes.

I grinned at him. "I simply escorted a pretty cop by car."

The detective slammed his fists on the table, getting right in my face. "You smashed her in the head. She died from brain swelling because of that blow."

"I'm sorry. Can you confirm the autopsy report, detective?" I said, smiling, knowing good and well no one ever found that cop. She was sleeping with the fish, and as all great criminals know—no body, no crime.

Quinn's face scowled.

Also, he knew I had more than enough money to get bail for a measly assault and kidnapping charge if it even stuck. It was his word against mine. No camera footage could be recovered on the night of the abduction. The unfortunate power outage for the surrounding shops and my club made sure of that. However, he may have had me on that murder charge.

"We also have a laundry list of other crimes you were involved in," he continued, that good boy mask sliding back into place.

I snorted. "I believe the words you're looking for are 'alleged crimes.' "

Guard dog took a deep breath through his nose.

"We have a witness."

I raised my eyebrows. Surprise was not something I liked to have in these situations with the law.

"You have someone claiming they saw me do all these bad man things?" I said, actual curiosity betraying my voice.

At my question, my heart stopped. The door opened, and stepping inside was my breathtaking obsession. Her pale blonde hair twirled up in a bun. Makeup coating her fair skin, but some red and purple tints shining through.

"This is Criminal Analyst Ella Fox," Quinn said.

My brain pounded like a drum, Ella?

Remembering the hospital visit, I recalled reading on her discharge paperwork, 'Ella.'

But I figured it to be an alias. She was protecting herself. My jaw dropped as my Little Shadow placed herself on the chair across from me. Her haunting gray eyes flashed in my mind and all the times I'd looked into them.

"Ella saw you assault me," Quinn said.

Ember—No, Ella stared at me curiously.

"She is the one who will arrest you. CSA Fox, the prisoner is yours to question."

I stared at the woman. My heart squeezed in my chest. Her presence seared me like a rusted blade in my heart.

"Lucius," she said. My name on her lips always sounded so lyrical, like a lullaby. Now, it was cold, hesitant, but calculative. She betrayed me.

I fell in fucking love with a cop.

One who must be undercover?

But that didn't make sense. Undercover cops didn't murder perps. They caught them.

So why….

"You are aware of your charges," she said, putting a stray light blonde hair behind her ear. "Do you have any questions before processing? I see you've forfeited your right to a lawyer to be your representative."

I simply stared at her.

The woman I've loved and hated for years has been chasing me all this time? The princess tricking me into tasting her poison? To become addicted? Anger, pain, betrayal, and confusion swirled in my eyes. Every emotion, every word said to her in my eyes, but one.

"Why?" I finally said.

She studied me, her beautiful eyes wide, unsure, and curious. How could she act like she didn't even know me? That I was just some criminal. My black heart shrunk. Anger took over, and rage like a burning fire was all I could see.

I barely heard the enforcers read me my rights. I did hear how I would be transported tomorrow to a high-security level containment. I would be refused bail and a pending trial for multiple other crimes linked to me.

All I could see was the damning eyes of the one I loved, who had watched me, who had caught me, and who would watch as I died from her poisonous kiss.

Chapter 31

Ember

I woke up on a park bench. My body hurt so badly that it was like a train ran over me, and then passengers on the train decided to jump on my face on the way out the door. Lucius was going to be upset that I wasn't in bed. He'd likely punish me for it, but honestly, I had to admit I didn't think I'd mind too badly.

He was somewhat of a lovable psycho...maybe even my lovable psycho.

He promised me we'd find the chief. Get answers about where the leader of all this shit was, and then it would be over. I could live free from all my pain, never having to shed any more blood.

Stretching and looking around, I realized I wasn't close to Lucius's club. I had fallen asleep next to a police station. The last thing I needed was to be seen by the dirty cops. They were probably wondering where one of their little piggies had gone by now.

I thought about that man—the good-looking cop. He wasn't bad to look at it. He was too good for my taste. He looked like the type who wanted to whisper sweet nothings into your ear while fucking you missionary by candlelight all night. Not bad, but not me.

Lucius had admitted that he'd accidentally killed the good-looking cop's partner. How? I don't know, but I'm guessing it wasn't great because the cop looked murderous when I'd watched him sizing up Lucius as I hid behind him.

He had crazy blue eyes like the color of the sky. I would remember those eyes anywhere, which was why I ducked behind the street bench, staring toward the police station as a man with a sling, dark blond hair, and those eyes walked toward a white car.

Oh my god. Did Lucius lose the prisoner? Did he escape? Was Lucius okay?

Tailing the cop, I waited in the shadows, my black hoodie firmly pulled up around my face and hair. There were two more police officers walking with a dark-haired man in orange wearing handcuffs.

My heart sank.

It was Lucius!

Trying to keep pace and remain unseen, I returned to the police cruisers and jimmied open the lock of the one farthest in the shadows, an older model that would allow me to hot wire it quickly. Driving a few miles behind, I carefully followed the direction of the white van, the two police cars, and the ex-captive cop following behind.

It felt like these boys had taken me on a whirlwind chase, the radio crackling with their pointless chatter as we went well past the town. Finally, I got a break when someone hopped on the radio and said, "Boys, I need to make a stop. Haven't taken a leak since roll call."

Crackling and laughter followed along with, "Okay, Bleu, pull up to the next gas station."

Following the police car, I pulled off to the side, making sure the shadows hid their old-time police cruiser.

"Don't take all day. I don't want this fucker getting any ideas," the cop said. The uniformed cop parked the white van in a spot that would make it too fucking hard to jack.

The cop was leaning against the back door, guarding his captive.

"Damnit," I muttered, irritation flooding me.

Slugging my hoodie off my head, trying to appear more civilian and less like a murderer, I ducked behind the cars and made my way inside the gas station. I turned and headed toward the back, where the bathroom and storage area was. The lock was flipped to red for the bathroom, and ungodly noises came from it. There was one guy down.

Ewe...

I hid behind a cardboard box. The contents of different candies and chips yet to be put up from the day's shipment sat beside it. The other cop patrolled the area, groaning at the smell, waving his arm, and coughing as he passed the door.

A chip bag crinkled, the sound giving away my location and causing me to freeze.

Cop number three stopped his coughing. With furrowed eyebrows, he walked over to me. My brain scrambled as I just stood there, and my entire body became visible to the police officer as he walked fully into the storage room.

"Oh, for fucks sake," he shouted, slapping his leg and laughing. "You scared me! I didn't know you were on."

His continued words confused me, but I smiled weakly, my face ashen with fear. I had one chance to save Lucius. One.

"You couldn't get enough of the action, huh? Had to see him go down, too?"

I nodded, not knowing what else to do. The man laughed again, stopping when his phone buzzed.

Flipping it open, he answered. "Ragen here."

I tried to walk away, but he held up a finger, mouthing to me to 'hold on.'

"Yeah! Hey Quinn, you'll never guess who wanted to tag along. She stowed away."

My eyes grew wide, and I smashed my fist into the cop's face, his body going down with a thud. His phone clattered on the ground.

The other man's faint "Hello" was audible as I took off out the back.

Waiting for the perfect second, I watched as the officer continued to call for the fallen officer. His irritation and worry grew until he finally bolted off, ran into the front door, and finally left the van's back entrance unguarded.

Not thinking about who might see me, I ran to the back and smashed the doors open.

Lucius was sitting on the metal bench, his orange jumpsuit and metal handcuffs gleaming in the sunlight.

His eyes moved toward me, and without a shred of emotion, he looked back to his feet.

What the fuck? Why was he mad at me?

Okay, so sleepwalking into the street was something I'd done, and I left him alone apparently to be arrested, but that wasn't my fault. Going to him and fussing with the pin to unlatch the cuffs, I stared into his eyes.

Emotionless.

Cold.

"Lucius!" I shook him, trying to get any amount of emotion.

He glared at me. The slight movement to his eyes, his rage burning me, that hateful stare made me step back.

"Lucius, we have to go!" I said, pulling him along with me.

His big body was dead weight as I dragged him out of the van's back door. Completely exposed, I used my full strength to haul him to the squad car. People at the pumps were giving me stares at my helpless grunting.

"Move your heavy ass!" I demanded, kicking him in the back of the leg.

He harrumphed but fell through the door's frame, landing on the seat. I couldn't get his cuffs off, but at least he was safe. Cursing, I watched the front entrance. All three of the cops walked out and headed for the van. Two of them hopped in their own cars, but the last one.

"Quinn," he was called, hopped out of the van, and went to the back, ripping the doors open and growling.

Shoving Lucius down in the seat, I started the car and dared one last look at the van.

Bad move.

His gaze caught mine. Shock and anger mingled into one as he ran toward us, yelling. I peeled the squad car out of the lot, the cop's words blurring as we sped away.

Chapter 32

Lucius

I stared at the woman driving like a bat out of hell beside me.

What the fuck was going on?

"How did you get captured?" she said, looking at me with icy savagery in her eyes.

I didn't speak. Just stared at her. Watched her pale finger flex on the steering wheel, weaving and turning expertly. She avoided areas she knew would be policed.

"Did the prisoner escape?" she continued, only making me blink at the fluency of lying.

My head throbbed from the bottle. My expensive vodka was ruined by her betrayal. Again, I stayed quiet.

"Lucius!" she yelled, whipping her head to me, her wild pale blonde hair curling and wet. My Little Shadow looked like an angel. But she was the devil—a betraying beast.

"Please," she begged, her eyes going blurry with unshed tears. "Why won't you talk to me?"

My silence stretched. She sighed, biting her lip until it bled and letting the tears fall.

"I know you feel betrayed," she started. Her hand was wiping angrily at her face. "But you have to know I can't help it!"

She all but screamed, whipping wildly on the road, the motion making me sway into her shoulder. I grunted, trying to push myself back up with my shoulder, but the bumps in the road kept me against her.

"I swear I never would have left. I don't know what happened. I've always been like that."

That made me pause. What was she even talking about? Studying her face, I searched her eyes. There was not a shred of anything but worry, guilt, and anger. Did she not feel like she had a choice in arresting me? Was her goal ruined by her feelings getting in the way?

My silence continued. She slammed the brakes, the car squealed to a sliding stop and slammed me into the door. She hid us under a bridge. The visibility was next to nothing around her because the fog was incredibly thick, making it look like snow.

"C'mon," she wiped again at her cheeks and grabbed the center of the cuffs to pull me out her door.

I allowed her, this time not dragging my feet but walking with her. If she was going to return me to the police now, it would look badly on us both, but then who the fuck was she?

"Who are you?" I decided to ask.

She rolled her eyes, pulling me faster down a set of stairs, a cheery red boat coming into view. The side of the boat read, "My princess."

She shuffled around inside a lockbox hidden under the boat seat and popped off the top with the lock combination that she'd entered without hesitation. Inside, she grabbed a boat key and started the ignition. Firing it up and not looking back, she drove the boat far from the cop car.

"Take off your clothes," she demanded.

Usually, I'd smirk at her, make her work for it, maybe tease her. But right now, I truly didn't know who the fuck I was looking at.

"I said take them off," she yelled, popping a knife from her belt, bringing the blade down on my chest, and slicing the orange jumpsuit. She nicked my skin.

Blood welled, and I accepted the burn, letting the torment of her betrayal seep away with the pain. She stared at me, tossing the ruined blob of orange overboard, and took the vessel in a different direction toward the bay.

"You won't talk to me, but you want me to hurt you?" she said with an exasperated sigh, watching as my body shivered.

I turned my head from her, moving my arms to my side, bashing the metal cuffs on a hook on the top of the outer edge of the boat, but they didn't break. Putting the machine into auto-pilot, she charged at me. Her icy rage made me feel cold.

"What the fuck Lucius?" she screamed at me, striking me across the face. Her pointy nails scraped across my cheek.

I hissed, my anger growing and catching her icy stare with my fiery one.

"You hurt me enough, Ella," I screamed back at her.

She froze, genuine confusion taking over her face. "What are you talking about?" Her words were a whisper—a wary, fragile tone.

"You tell me, porthos," I spat, not buying her rouse.

She shook her head, those tears forming again in her blue-gray eyes.

"No," she said, that tone still fragile but more firm. "What are you talking about, Lucius?"

I studied her again and watched her eyes, fierce, angry, hurt, and confused. There were no lies in them. There was nothing but true sadness and confusion.

"I don't understand," I said, my thoughts racing.

She took a lighter from her pocket, flicking it, trying to hide the wind from extinguishing its light.

"I know you feel betrayed." She brought the lighter toward my hands. "I know I left when you needed me."

The lighter burned the chains, the heat searing my wrists for a minute before something came down hard on the center and cracked it wide. The two handcuffs were now separated. I could strangle her, kill her, and toss her to the watery depths. Looking at her neck and feeling my fingers twitch, she walked up to me.

Picking up my hands and placing them around her neck in the exact spot I was just eyeing, she said, "If you need to kill me because I hurt you…because I betrayed your trust and wasn't there when you needed me, fine. But Lucius, know this…"

I stared into her eyes.

Nothing but truth shone in their depths as she whispered, "I love you."

Chapter 33

Ember

*L*ucius blinked, his grip not tightening or loosening.
Simply frozen.

"I love you," I repeated, ready to live with my shame of betrayal or die without him.

He opened his mouth to speak. Opened and closed it. Then he finally whispered, "Why did you give me up? Why did you choose him?"

I furrowed my brow. I had no clue what he meant. I would never choose anyone over him. I didn't give him up, I fell victim to my own mind.

"I didn't?" I said, unsure and cautious. "Lucius, I'm sorry. I was asleep, and I woke up in the park. I didn't know you were taken."

He frowned, shaking his head, his confusion and anger growing as he watched my eyes so intently.

"I sometimes sleepwalk…" I mumbled, trying to help him understand, ashamed to admit it out loud. Doing so made the power of the curse grip me tighter. Define me.

"You…what?" He took his hands away from my throat and ran his hands through his hair the way he did when he was frustrated or stressed.

"Yes," I continued and shrugged. "I've done it since I was a teenager after…" I let my words trail off, not wanting to relive the horror of that night. "I was taken," I stated numbly, "By drug dealers…they tortured me. Tried to rip me apart for their drugs."

He sat silent, waiting for me to continue.

"There were two of them. One was a really bad tweaker. He was chaotic, out of his mind, but I managed to kill him." My words were like vomit, flowing from my mouth without permission.

"I escaped the place they took me to and ran into the night, but the druggie caught me. He smashed me onto the ground, but I killed him. I killed him with some broken plastic from his taillight. I busted the taillight when they grabbed me. I kicked it."

The words continued to flow.

"The other guy wasn't high at all. He was calculative and smart, and he wanted something. I think he was trying to train the druggie. But I stole the car, hotwired it, and ended up in a ditch."

Lucius reached for my hand. Stroking his thumb over it as I continued letting the tears I'd kept hidden for so many years fall freely.

"I don't remember anything after that, just that I wasn't going to let anyone hurt me again. I knew I would be strong, and I'd kill every last one of these zombie addicts."

"You've never killed an innocent," he said, wincing. "Until you met me," he continued, watching my tears continue to fall. The salty taste of them blended with the tangy air.

"Until you," I agreed, sitting down on his lap, unable to stand it any longer. He smoothed my hair, the wind whipping it wildly around.

"But then, why did you arrest me?" he said. "Why were you with them?"

I blinked, my anger and confusion were not able to compute the words he was speaking.

"I have no idea what you are talking about," I said from exhaustion. "I wasn't with anyone. I came to save you as soon as I found out!"

"But—" He stopped, his mind visibly spinning, and his gaze bounced between my eyes.

"That's why," he said at last. "That's why I couldn't find you for so long. Because you weren't you."

I was starting to think the police had gotten rough with Lucius. Maybe they'd hit his head. He did have a ton of bruises and scrapes.

Frowning, I put my hands on his cheeks. "Are you okay?"

He locked my hand in his, sighing a long breath before he spoke. "I need you to take us somewhere."

Arriving at the apartment Lucius had directed me to find, I didn't know what he was doing or what this place was to him. Going to the door, a nice man walked out and greeted me, holding it open. Clearly, strangers didn't care who walked into their homes, which was insanely odd to me, but whatever.

Arriving at the designated door, I stared at the grooved mark on the handle. A strange humming feeling started in my body. Not knowing exactly how, I reached up and grabbed a key from the top ledge of the door, staring at the key in bewilderment as I unlocked then turned the knob.

Immediately, two cats ran toward my feet—a fluffy, huge white one and the little black kitten from the alley. Lucius followed behind me, latching the door shut and watching me as I looked at the place.

I felt the weird humming again. This time, it was amped up to a buzz in my head. It was giving me a headache. Everywhere I looked, a ghostly feeling of what felt like a memory played in my head.

The couch that sat against the window, I knew there was a red wine stain on the left cushion underneath. The bed that was placed along the far wall, I knew the covers came from a garage sale on Sax Street, and in the kitchen, I knew there was a PBJ on the top shelf.

My head buzzed louder, my hands reaching up to grip my skull —the buzzing was so loud. My confusion and panic rose as I blindly looked around the room. My vision seemed to fade in and out like a filter on a phone.

Staggering into a wall, I heard the sound of glass shattering, a picture frame falling to the ground and sending shards scattered around my feet. Kneeling down, I grabbed the photo that was laid down. I flipped it over and stared at the two people.

I saw myself—happy, playful, and smiling, but I didn't remember this. I didn't know where I was. The person beside me had curly brown hair, red lips, and a kind teasing smile. This was that girl. This was…

I screamed, my mind splintering in two. My vision went dark. Blinking, I saw my hands coated in blood. Blinking again, I saw myself hugging a stranger…no, a cop. Flashing again and again, I saw only the images as they flowed into my mind.

Conversations, people, Quinn, my friend, my partner.

The battle between him and Lucius.

My own hands as they brought down a bottle on his head.

More memories, more blood, and my nose began to drip red onto my hands, splattering all over the picture, making everything appear as if it were covered in a bright red haze.

Cassie.

My sister.

My beautiful sister.

I screamed again, thrashing as the images continued to invade my mind, ripping me into two and shattering my heart, ruining my sense of self.

"I killed her," I whispered, my teeth chattering so badly I could barely see straight. Lucius was there, trying to hold me, trying to calm me down.

"I killed her," I repeated, my tears and blood mingling as it distorted the image of Cassie's face on the picture below me.

Her look of shock and pain flashed before my eyes. Her strength to fight, her bravery… her death.

"I killed her," I said again. Louder. Broken. Agonized, "I killed my sister!"

My world shattered.

I wasn't a person.

I was a monster.

I was a liar, a fake, a completely broken doll.

The dealers. Their faces. All their faces flashed before my eyes like flipping cards, names, and profiles on paper, to their screams and blood dripping from their bodies.

I did that. I killed them. I killed all of them.

I was chasing…myself.

The reason why I could never find any trace of Snow White was because it was my own reflection. My own hands. My own kills. Lucius was rocking me back and forth, humming a strange Russian lullaby in my ears. My pain made me feel raw, the horror at what I'd done—the blood on my hands.

My sister.

Cassie.

Gone because of me.

Killed…because of me.

Sobs wracked my whole body, making my aches feel like I was physically separating from my physical form.

Snow White, I thought about the mantra in my head.

Cassie.

Me.

I couldn't focus. I couldn't stop the never-ending sickness in my soul. It was like black water that felt like it was drowning me.

The blood I'd spilled.

The blood I'd enjoyed spilling—all of it, all the years and memories poisoning me.

Chapter 34

Lucius

I watched Ember…Ella. I watched the love of my life as she broke and cried her soul into the ground. Her sobs convulsed her body as her own memories repeatedly attacked her. I never understood until now why I'd never been able to catch her, why my Little Shadow was like a ghost. But now it made sense—all of her connections and habits.

I never followed her unless she was chasing down prey. Could I have saved her from this pain had I known the truth sooner?

I saw my Little Shadow go to this apartment once. Thinking it was probably someone's place she was hunting, I ignored it, writing it off as unimportant. But the night I saw Ella at the art gallery with that guy, I followed her home. She passed out by my dumpsters that night, making sure the whole neighborhood knew she was there.

After she had woken up and started walking, it was the apartment she went to, but she never made it. Those fucking assholes had gotten to her. Ripping her red dress to shreds and knocking her out.

I'd been so angry that I hadn't been close by, taking too long to find where they took her. Those vital moments were a mess in my mind as I had blindly searched for her in those tunnels.

Rubbing her hair now, I looked at her, letting my lips trail down her cheek, her jaw, her neck. Letting her know I was here and that I was irrevocably hers.

"Cassie," she whispered on repeat.

Cassie was the unfortunate girl that Markus got his slimy hooks into—she was the one he liked and took up to Boston. The one that my Little Shadow killed in order to save my life. That girl had been her sister.

I knew that she was related to a cop, but I never would have dreamed that the cop was my Little Shadow. The door swung open, and I jolted. The plaster puffed out on the sides as it smacked the wall and stayed embedded into it. My senses were muted from my worry for my Little Shadow.

Four men barged inside, and all of them had on police uniforms. None of them were the cops from earlier.

"Well, well, well," one of them said—an authority booming from him as his men flanked his sides.

I shielded Ella, her body not so much as moving. Her sobs still had control of her.

"I mean, really," the man continued. "I never would have thought to play out this fun little story—the cop falls for the killer?"

I glared at him. My body was unable to do anything but protect her from their gazes. Plus, I knew if I walked away from her, they could hurt her.

"Awe, little Ella," he crooned, stepping forward and roaring as the two cats ran and attacked his legs.

Hissing and puffing up, the little black one scratched his thigh to ribbons, the two bolting away when he swung his arm angrily at them.

"Go skin them," the boss ordered a guard to his left.

The man looked at his bleeding leg and hesitated.

"Uh…boss?" he said, looking off down the hallway where the two cats fled.

"Yes, you…you buffoon! Now!"

Reaching into my boot, I grabbed one of my knives and tossed it straight into the eye of the "Buffoon," watching his body plop loudly onto the ground.

The little felines were long gone now, hopefully safe outside the apartment. Ella would never forgive me if something happened to anyone else she loved. I knew that for a fact, and her little cats did come to her rescue after all.

"Interesting," the boss said, eyeing me suspiciously. "Could it be that the killer loves his captor back?"

Chuckling and grabbing my knife from the dead guy's eye, he turned to his other lackey. "Get the male. Do whatever with the cop."

Steeling myself and trying to rouse Ella to no avail, I prepared myself for the lackey. His big arms hurled down with a baton he had grabbed from his side, and I felt it smashing into my back as I shielded what was mine.

"Don't ruin the package, you oaf. His Daddy needs him alive!" My vision went blurry as I gripped Ella tighter. The man chuckled. "He needs a little makeover. He's too pretty."

Grabbing a broken shard of glass, I jammed it into the guy's neck. Blood spurted onto my face and chest, the strain of this man's weight knocking me over. Grunting, I shoved at his body.

The boss took the opportunity to snatch Ella, flipping her up and off the ground and over his shoulder. Her head smashed into the entryway of the door, knocking her out cold. He squished her in his arms, her head lolling to the side. I scrambled out from underneath the lackey, rushing at the leader.

"Ah, ah, ah…" he said, halting my movements when he brought my knife up to Little Shadow's throat.

"You come with me, boy, willingly and without all this fussing. If you don't, I'll slit the pretty girl's throat and make you watch as I spill every drop of her blood onto you."

I paled, my options obsolete. I couldn't rush him because he would have time to kill her. I couldn't throw something at him because he'd get angry and kill her. I didn't have a choice if I wanted my Snow White to live.

I had to go with him and surrender.

"Fine!" I said, putting my hands up and watching the knife hover over her neck. "But you have to let her go."

The man smiled, yellow teeth gleaming. "Oh, on the contrary, little prince…." he said, taking a dangerous step toward me. "I think our king would like to meet the princess, don't you? Hmm, our murderous little Snow White."

Chapter 35

Ella

Waking up, I looked around. Black bars were blocking my vision.

What the fuck?

My world was broken. My reality was so shifted that I couldn't comprehend anything. Feeling a lump on the back of my head the size of a rock, I groaned. I honed in on the noises I was hearing. Was that…grunting? Yes, it was, and a whip.

"Lucius," I said, trying to snap out of my hazed stupor.

I had to pull myself together and accept whatever was left of myself. I had to think. I had to use both parts of myself to get out of this. Ella would look at it tactically, finding any holes in the structure. Walking around and feeling the wall, I cursed. There was hay littering the area, covering cedar-looking boards underneath me and steel bars. The cell was about ten feet wide and went to the top of what looked like a barn.

I was in a barn?

Okay, so a barn…It didn't matter where I was. I needed to find a way out. Maybe this box was a part of a stall, but maybe there was something here I could use. The sounds of the whip cracking made my stomach roll. Lucius sounded so pained, so tired, and so close that he had to be on the other side of the wall from me.

"Tell us, Lucius, and this all goes away," someone said.

Lucius's resounding "Fuck you" was laced with pain and rage.

Tell him what?

Another time. I had work to do.

Getting on my hands and knees, I shuffled through the hay, scraping my knee on some shattered glass. It looked like an old lamp had been broken. I picked up a piece, and it was the kind of lamp that was filled with oil!

Looking up at a window, I could clearly see the rays of the sun. The light streamed down on the wall. The line was straight and sure. I reached up, hissing when my flesh felt like it was sizzling.

With a smile on my face, I held the glass because this was what Ember would do. I was going to watch this place burn. Reaching up to angle the shard of glass at the lantern's wick, I put it in the sunlight. Feeling a sense of elation as a tiny whisp of black smoke licked the wick and puffed into an ember, I watched it grow and glow vibrantly.

Hopping down from the little wooden table, I grabbed the lantern and began scooting the hay with my foot to the side of the stall.

The whipping sounds increased. Lucius's grunts had turned into genuine cries now.

I had to hurry.

Making a small stack of hay toward the back of the stall, I blew on the wick. The embers flickered and fell onto the heap. A small spark popped, burying into the haystack, and a tiny pattern of black smoke began rising into the air.

Kneeling down, I blew more life into the ember. I watched it turn into an orange, a red, and soon a full fire bloomed. The black smoke rose up in a cloud, bouncing off the ceiling and thrown back down. Within minutes, I was coughing, the hazy orange glow making my vision blurry.

"What the fuck?" someone yelled, running as I hid behind the wooden hatch. They opened the cell door, and I attacked. Not thinking, I just threw the man into the flames. He screamed, swatting at his body while I happily watched his face melt.

Horrified at what I had done, I shook my head, bolting out of the cell door and running toward the sound of the cracking whip.

There were no animals in here, thank god—just pounds of money, which meant there was a ton of paper for the fire to burn. Lucius was strung up on an awful-looking contraption. His chest was bare, with ribbons of flesh chewed all over his skin from the whip. My eyes focused on the blood as it dripped to the ground, and my anger turned to a red haze.

The man in front of him wouldn't see me coming. Grabbing the whip from his hands and wrapping it into a noose around his neck, I pulled, watching Lucius's eyes as I did. Quickly, the man went limp under my grip.

Lucius's wild eyes found mine. I tried to smile at him as I released his binds from the machine that held him up, leading him to the exit doors.

Smoke was so thick now that it was hard even to see him, even though he was right next to me. However, the world around us was shaded with shades of black and orange.

"Who are you?" he said to me.

"I don't know," I said in truth, finally finding the doors to the barn and smashing them open with our bodies.

"Awe," I heard from the forest area surrounding the barn. "How cute. Looks like the princess saves the prince."

I glared at the man, my anger turning my veins to ice.

"Too bad we need to kill you," he mused, making a face that said he didn't actually care.

"Too bad you think you actually can," I replied, searching for more of them in the shadows.

There wasn't—just bodies that looked shredded up by an animal. Lucius had fought. He had fought, and they must have threatened me because, otherwise, they would all be dead. The haze cleared the further we moved away from the barn. I could make out the speaker now. It was my shady police chief.

Was Quinn in on this? Was his body amongst these men?

I couldn't think like that.

I had to get out and get Lucius to safety. Chief Doger paced around a field, an insanity set in his brown eyes.

"You're a crafty one, Ella," he said, facing me. "I never knew you were the killer all this time."

I decided not to mention that I didn't either because what would be the point?

"You wouldn't notice something right underneath your nose the whole time because your face is too far shoved up your ass! You are no Alyosha—leader of the Bratva," Lucius growled, his voice low.

"I failed the king. I did," Doger said with a sad sigh. "You see, he wanted me to find the princess. I found a princess! Just not thee princess."

Lucius and I exchanged a look because the man was speaking in mad circles.

"I was to be the king's guard. I was to get the castle," he whined, stomping his foot like a child.

Carefully, Lucius and I walked forward, slowly making our way toward the mad chief.

"He said I'm weak, you know," he wailed. "Said he wasn't gracing me with his presence!"

Lucius had something in his hands. A small object. An apple? He gave him a look, and he winked at me when we were finally a few inches from the crazed man.

"Oh mighty lord, you were wronged!" Lucius said, his head bowing and his torn-up body wincing. Following suit, I bowed as well. "You should have the castle."

We looked into the eyes of a very drugged-up male. I wasn't sure what he was on, but observing it was terrifying. There was a familiarity to his actions that I couldn't shake.

"Yes..." the man moaned, tears streaming from his reddened eyes, his hands wobbly with a vial filled with something in his grip.

"I should be the king!"

Lucius nodded, walking up to the man and patting him on the back. He reached around and snatched the vial from the chief's hand. His 'sleight of hand act' worked.

Flashing me another look and a wink, Lucius continued the charade. "Ah, but you are the king."

Chief Doger's drugged eyes locked on me, his yellow teeth grinning with unformed, tainted thoughts waiting to be spoken.

"I'm the king," he agreed. "And I'll take that princess."

Lucius flinched slightly, his composure cracking like a mirror.

"Of course," he said, smiling the fakest smile I'd ever seen on his face. "But first, a gift for you, my king."

Holding the apple high in the air, I could see a frothy, white liquid bubbling inside a small hole. Lucius caught my gaze once more, giving me a genuine smile. Out of the corner of my eye, I saw a car roll up beside the barn—an army of men got out and stormed toward us.

Lucius's face paled. His gaze was focused toward the head of the group, on a male that looked so much like Ivy that I had to blink to catch up.

This had to be Lucius's father.

This was my mark.

The one I'd fought so hard to kill.

"Alyosha," I growled. Alyosha's men formed an impenetrable line beside him.

Smirking, he looked at me. "Have we met?"

"No, or you'd already be dead," I said.

Alyosha laughed. His thick, accented tone was so familiar it felt strange. "You've found yourself a leach, my son." His tone was cool, unattached.

Lucius glared fiery daggers at his father, but he didn't say a word. He just stared at his father with a look of hatred.

"We're on a time crunch. Unfortunately, a police officer who had been forced off my payroll caught wind of this and is headed in this direction," he stated.

Quinn?

The men walked forward, grabbing my arm and pulling me from Lucius's side, dragging me back to the burning barn.

"No! I'm the king," Chief Doger shrieked. "You can't have it!"

Lucius was stoically silent as Alyosha unsheathed a huge sword, slicing off the chief's head in one fluid motion. Then, his head fell to the ground with a squelching noise. The hands of the guards were firm, my efforts not making a dent as I fought to free myself.

Lucius was fighting them now. He was slashing their bodies into shreds, his bare fists ripping out their hearts, lungs, and entrails. His father simply watched him tear down six of his soldiers. Two of the soldiers were still dragging me. One of them threw open the door to the barn. The smoke billowed out, the heat singing my skin as we got closer and closer.

The two guards locked their arms around mine, throwing us down into the hay at the farthest corner of the barn. The one place it wasn't a blazing inferno.

They were sent here to die—their last task was to hold me down as I burned. I looked around, only seeing the black and red fire surrounding me.

Was Lucius okay?

Was his father going to kill him?

What about Quinn? What would he do when he got here?

Would he be safe?

What could I do? I had to help them. I had to get out to get free.

I didn't know who I was anymore. How could I help anyone? Who did they need?

Who was I?…

Ember?

Ella?

Nobody?

No!

I was both Ella and Ember, but also neither of them.

Swinging my head back and contacting the left guy's face, he'd loosened his grip enough for me to pull free. Using him as a catapult to roll over the other guy's chest and fling the first into the wall, a pile of burning hay fell onto him as he crashed into the wall.

The other guy fought. Snapping my wrist with insane efficiency, pain, and rage blinded me. I couldn't give up.

I had to think. How could I get out of here?

I couldn't be just Ella or just Ember. They both have weaknesses. I needed to accept myself. Accept that I was not just Ella or Ember, but both of them. Coming to terms with this made me feel empowered and nauseous. I would never get used to my sense of justice being so divided. I thought about my training as Ella. The hours I spent sparring with Quinn, all the protocols and knowledge on safety, and especially the anatomy of the human body.

Cracking his skull with the back of my head as the sparring had taught me, I kicked my feet off the wall, jumping behind him, the motion so fluid he didn't catch it in time.

Truly, I had to accept both parts of me to make this work.

What would Ember do? Find a weak point and use it to my advantage.

Using the skills and mindset I'd learned as Ember, I focused up, and I could see a beam through the smoke. It was over the head of the man. I ran up his body and propelled myself off his abdomen to jump up and grab onto a beam, spinning his body into an open flame.

The fire from the hay was licking up the entirety of the floor now. The smoke was rising and making my lungs burn. I wouldn't make it. I was going to burn alive, and if Lucius died out there without my help, I would let the flames claim me.

The soldier burned below me, and his screams were a promise of my soon-to-come fate as the flames licked higher into the air.

My arms burned.

My body singed with the heat.

My every muscle seized with pain.

No, I was not going out like this.

I forced my arms to pull my body up and crawl onto the top of the barn, crawling on my forearms and dragging my feet behind me. I couldn't see a thing, afraid I'd slip any second and fall to my death.

But then, I felt the cool, smooth texture of glass. Angling myself, I took a deep breath and smashed my foot into the panel.

Chapter 36

Lucius

he blood dripped down my chest, skin, organs, and everything decorating the inside of a human body was plastered to me like glue. My father stood watching as his shiny toy was mauling all of his soldiers. I looked at the barn. My heart sank. Clouds of black were billowing from every crevice.

She was dead.

The man who took it all away from me had taken her, too.

Roaring to the sky, I slammed into my father.

His precision in fighting was so untouched that I felt like I was dancing and losing. My body was smashed and bashed and slammed onto the ground. Sweat poured from me, anger lacing my every cell.

"You killed her," I screamed, trying to ram into him and roaring louder as he dodged me.

His soldiers were good. Their blows were all precise and strong, but my father was on another level. His blows were pinpointed with such precise points on my body, and the pain was so blinding that I felt bewitched by a curse.

"Love blinds a man," he scoffed, twirling around as he dodged my wrath again.

"You loved Mother!"

He missed a step, allowing my fist to slam into his face.

Shaking off the blow, he straightened. "Love weakens a man."

I frowned.

How could he dismiss my mother? How could he pretend she was just a weakness?

"No," I yelled, facing off with him again, my pain at the loss of my Little Shadow fueling my body.

"Love shows you your own strength." His arm snapping left a satisfying crunch as his body slammed to the ground. I pounced on him before he could move, my Little Shadow's dagger in my palm.

"This is for Eili," I screamed, slashing a gash on his outstretched arm.

"This is for Mother!" A large line opened his forearm.

Raising the blade above his heart, I said, "This is for my Kayeten!"

But my hand stalled as an ashen form hurled out of the second-story window to the ground.

Alyosha didn't hesitate, smashing me in the face and running from my grasp.

I heard him running, his body bleeding and weakened. I could kill him. I could chase him down and end this.

But…

My gaze landed on the heap on the ground—the soot-covered form was bloodied and unmoving. Running as fast as my body would carry me, I dropped to the form. There was so much soot and ash that I could barely even make out my Little Shadow. Her blonde hair blackened, her body crumpled.

"No, no, no!" I cradled her and rubbed the ash from her face.

She was not breathing.

"No!"

My tears blinded me as they dripped down onto her coated

cheek. I breathed air into her lungs, pumping her chest again and again. The motions blurred as I continued over and over to breathe life into the one thing keeping me alive. She sputtered, her body jolting up and coughing. She got up, and ash fell from her body. Her features were more visible the more she shook. She coughed again and again, but she was breathing.

"Lucius." Her voice was raspy. It had to be painful and sore.

I shushed her, holding her close to me.

"Yes, I am here E—" I stopped, unsure what to call her.

"I'm no one," she said, looking around sadly, her tears unshed. I looked at her. Her body was covered in ashes from head to toe, and soot coated her face and hair. I began to chuckle and she was startled, unaware of what I saw.

Kissing her filthy cheek, I smiled. "Baby, you are not no one. You may not be Ella or Ember." I told her, and her face fell, but picking up her chin, I continued, "But you, sweetheart, have literally risen from the ashes. You are born anew."

I paused. "You are my Phoenix."

With her eyes wide, I kissed her deeply.

Pheonix

I stalked in the shadows with Lucius by my side. His warmth cocooning me in the darkness, Quinn was in the window. The bright look on his face was a joy to see. He was being promoted tonight. He was the new chief. Finally, we had a good human in charge who wasn't bat-shit mad. They were placing a medal on his shirt, mouthing words I couldn't hear, but I knew he was telling the crowd of Micah Quinn's heroic achievement of catching the Snow White killer.

They were now explaining how he found the suspect at an abandoned barn, how the notorious serial killer had committed suicide and finally met her own end in a fiery blaze. Also, drugs from the cartel were littered around the area, and an apple was lying at the scene.

Everyone was shocked but Micah Quinn. Now, he was the head of the special victim's unit. The place he always wanted to be. The place to avenge his sister and find his own peace.

Smiling, I let Lucius pull me into his hot embrace. Giggling, I grabbed his hand and led him to the high school by the station.

It was easy enough to sneak into the pool area, and Lucius looked like a kid when he did a cannonball into the deep end. I laughed and traipsed around, letting him get a good look at me in my bra and panties. His eyes were heavy, and I could see his pants tenting under the water. Giggling, I made a 'come here' motion while lying on my back and spreading my legs open.

Lucius hummed his approval, which made me moan. His water-drenched body hopped up on the side, pulling him out of the pool. All but running to me, he flopped down and mounted me, his hard length pressing into my panties. Growling, he ripped them off, then dove onto my pussy. I felt his lips and his tongue working their magic. Letting out a moan, I ground into his face, riding the pleasure but pulling back right before I got there.

With a groan, he glared at me. "Why didn't you soak my face, love?"

I dropped my eyes to his, leaning and whispering in the most seductive voice, "I could, but are you wet from me or the pool?"

He smiled a dangerous smile, ready to bury his face back into my heat, but I took my foot and shoved him into the pool.

His body splashed from his awkward flip, and his sputtering gasp made me laugh out loud.

"Well…" I said, standing up and giving him my best devilish grin. "Looks like you're soaked now."

THE END

About the Author

SK Pryntz loves writing gritty, thrilling, dark tales that will twist you into knots until you can't stand it. Her love of writing began at an early age, as well as singing and reading about fairytales. However, as she has grown older, the real versions of the fairytales are sincerely her favorites.

When she surfaces from her writing cave, she loves spending time with her husband and children.

Thank You

Thank you to all those who decided to read my book.

Only with your continued support can independent authors like myself keep writing, which is why your reviews mean so much.

If you enjoyed this book, please consider leaving me a review.

I hope you love my psychos as much as I do.

Sincerely,

SK Pryntz

Stalk Me Links